Native American Tales and Legends

Edited by

ALLAN A. MACFARLAN

DOVER PUBLICATIONS, INC.
Mineola, New York

DOVER JUVENILE CLASSICS
EDITOR OF THIS VOLUME: KATHY CASEY

Copyright

Copyright © 1968 by The George Macy Companies, Inc.
All rights reserved.

Acknowledgments

The following stories in this volume are copyrighted:
"The Discovery of Fire" and "The Hermit Thrush" (Aren Akweks, Six Nations Museum, Onchiota, New York)
"The First False Face," "The Four Winds," and "The Loon's Necklace" (from *Indian Adventure Trails*, Allan Macfarlan, © 1953, Dodd, Mead and Company)
"The Mouse's Children" (from *By Cheyenne Campfires*, George Bird Grinnell, © 1926 Yale University Press)
"The Origin of the Buffalo and of Corn" (*Anthropological Papers of the Field Museum*)
"How the Earth Began" (*Bulletin of the American Museum of Natural History*)
Some stories in this book are retellings by George Bird Grinnell of legends included in his *Blackfoot Lodge Tales* and *Pawnee Hero Stories and Folk Tales*. Other stories are from Henry Rowe Schoolcraft's *The Myth of Hiawatha and Other Oral Legends of the North American Indians*. Tales collected by Dr. Franz Boas, by Frank H. Cushing, and by several others also are included.

Bibliographical Note

This Dover edition, first published in 2001, includes a selection of stories from *American Indian Legends*, published by The Heritage Press in 1968.

Library of Congress Cataloging-in-Publication Data

Macfarlan, Allan A.
    Native American tales and legends / [selected and] edited by Allan A. Macfarlan.
        p. cm. — (Dover juvenile classics)
    Rev. ed. of: American Indian legends. New York : Heritage Press, 1968.
    ISBN-13: 978-0-486-41476-8 (pbk.)
    ISBN-10: 0-486-41476-0 (pbk.)
    1. Indians of North America—Folklore. 2. Tales—North America. 3. Legends—North America. I. Macfarlan, Allan A. American Indian legends. II. Title. III. Series.
    E98.F6 M143 2000
    398.2'097—dc21

                                                            00–047374

Manufactured in the United States by Courier Corporation
41476008   2015
www.doverpublications.com

Contents

Nations and Tribes Represented

Most areas are within what now is the United States of America.

Micmac: Nova Scotia and the Maritime provinces of Canada
Tsimshian: north Pacific coast
Maidu: northeast California
Pueblo, Zuñi: southwest
Blackfoot, Cheyenne, Dakota, Pawnee: Great Plains
Cherokee, Choctaw, Shawnee: southeast
Iroquois, Mohawk, Onondaga, Seneca: the woodlands of upper
New York State and near the eastern Great Lakes, and in south-
ern Canada just north of those areas
Chippewa, Ojibwa, Ottawa: south-central Canada and the north-
central area of the valleys of the Mississippi and Ohio rivers

How the Earth Began

In the beginning there was no sun, no moon, no stars. All was dark, and everywhere there was only water. A raft came floating on the water. It came from the north, and in it were two persons—Turtle (Anosma) and Father-of-the-Secret-Society (Peheipe). The stream flowed very rapidly. Then from the sky a rope of feathers, called *Pokelma,* was let down, and down it came Earth-Initiate. When he reached the end of the rope, he tied it to the bow of the raft, and stepped in. His face was covered and was never seen, but his body shone like the sun. He sat down, and for a long time said nothing.

At last Turtle said, "Where do you come from?" and Earth-Initiate answered, "I come from above." Then Turtle said, "Brother, can you not make for me some good dry land, so that I may sometimes come up out of the water?" Then he asked another time, "Are there going to be any people in the world?" Earth-Initiate thought awhile, then said, "Yes." Turtle asked, "How long before you are going to make people?" Earth-Initiate replied, "I don't know. You want to have some dry land: well, how am I going to get any earth to make it of?" Turtle answered, "If you will tie a rock about my left arm, I'll dive for some."

Earth-Initiate did as Turtle asked, and then, reaching around, took the end of a rope from somewhere, and tied it to Turtle. When Earth-Initiate came to the raft, there was no rope there: he just reached out and found one.

1

Turtle said, "If the rope is not long enough, I'll jerk it once, and you must haul me up; if it is long enough, I'll give two jerks, and then you must pull me up quickly, as I shall have all the earth that I can carry." Just as Turtle went over the side of the boat, Father-of-the-Secret-Society began to shout loudly.

Turtle was gone a long time. He was gone six years; and when he came up, he was covered with green slime, he had been down so long. When he reached the top of the water, the only earth he had was a very little under his nails: the rest had all washed away. Earth-Initiate took with his right hand a stone knife from under his left armpit, and carefully scraped the earth out from under Turtle's nails. He put the earth in the palm of his hand, and rolled it about till it was round; it was as large as a small pebble. He laid it on the stern of the raft. By and by he went to look at it: it had not grown at all. The third time that he went to look at it, it had grown so that it could be spanned by the arms. The fourth time he looked, it was as big as the world, the raft was aground, and all around were mountains as far as he could see. The raft came ashore at Tadoiko, and the place can be seen today.

When the raft had come to land, Turtle said, "I can't stay in the dark all the time. Can't you make a light, so that I can see?" Earth-Initiate replied, "Let us get out of the raft, and then we will see what we can do." So all three got out. Then Earth-Initiate said, "Look that way, to the east! I am going to tell my sister to come up." Then it began to grow light, and day began to break; then Father-of-the-Secret-Society began to shout loudly, and the sun came up. Turtle said, "Which way is the sun going to travel?" Earth-Initiate answered, "I'll tell her to go this way, and go down there." After the sun went down, Father-of-the-Secret-Society began to cry and shout again, and it grew very dark. Earth-Initiate said, "I'll tell my brother to come up." Then the moon rose. Then Earth-Initiate asked Turtle and Father-of-the-Secret-Society, "How do you like it?" And they both answered, "It is very good." Then Turtle asked, "Is that all you are going to do for us?" and Earth-Initiate answered, "No, I am going to do more yet." Then he called the stars each by its name, and they came out.

When this was done, Turtle asked, "Now what shall we do?" Earth-Initiate replied, "Wait, and I'll show you." Then he made a tree grow at Tadoiko, the tree called *Hukimtsa*; and Earth-Initiate and Turtle and Father-of-the-Secret-Society sat in its shade for two days. The tree was very large, and had twelve different kinds of acorns growing on it.

After they had sat for two days under the tree, they all went off to see the world that Earth-Initiate had made. They started at sunrise, and were back by sunset. Earth-Initiate traveled so fast that all they could see was a ball of fire flashing about under the ground and the water. While they were gone, Coyote and his dog Rattlesnake came up out of the ground. It is said that Coyote could see Earth-Initiate's face. When Earth-Initiate and the others came back, they found Coyote at Tadoiko. All five of them then built huts for themselves, and lived there at Tadoiko, but no one could go inside of Earth-Initiate's house. Soon after the travelers came back, Earth-Initiate called the birds from the air, and made the trees and then the animals. He took some mud, and of this made first a deer; after that, he made all the other animals. Sometimes Turtle would say, "That does not look well: can't you make it some other way?"

Some time after this, Earth-Initiate and Coyote were at Estobusin Yamani. Earth-Initiate said, "I am going to make people." In the middle of the afternoon he began, for he had returned to Tadoiko. He took dark red earth, mixed it with water, and made two figures, one a man, and one a woman. He laid the man on his right side, and the woman on his left, inside his house. Then he lay down himself, flat on his back, with his arms stretched out. He lay thus and sweated all the afternoon and night. Early in the morning the woman began to tickle him in the side. He kept very still, and did not laugh. By and by he got up, thrust a piece of pitchwood into the ground, and fire burst out. The two people were very white. No one today is as white as they were. Their eyes were pink, their hair was black, their teeth shone brightly, and they were very handsome.

It is said that Earth-Initiate did not finish the hands of the people, as he did not know how it would be best to do it. Coyote saw the people, and suggested that they ought to have hands like his. Earth-Initiate said, "No, their hands shall be like mine." Then he finished them. When Coyote asked why their hands were to be like that, Earth-Initiate answered, "So that, if they are chased by bears, they can climb trees." The first man was called Kuksu, and the woman, Morning-Star Woman (La Idambulum Kule).

When Coyote had seen the two people, he asked Earth-Initiate how he had made them. When he was told, he thought, "That is not difficult. I'll do it myself." He did just as Earth-Initiate had told him, but could not help laughing, when, early in the morning, the woman poked him in the ribs. As a result of his failing to keep still, the people were glass-eyed. Earth-Initiate said, "I told you not to laugh," but Coyote declared he had not. This was the first lie.

By and by there came to be a good many people. Earth-Initiate had wanted to have everything comfortable and easy for people, so that none of them should have to work. All fruits were easy to obtain, no one was ever to get sick and die. As the people grew numerous, Earth-Initiate did not come as often as formerly, he only came to see Kuksu in the night. One night he said to him, "Tomorrow morning you must go to the little lake near here. Take all the people with you. I'll make you a very old man before you get to the lake." So in the morning Kuksu collected all the people, and went to the lake. By the time he had reached it, he was a very old man. He fell into the lake, and sank down out of sight. Pretty soon the ground began to shake, the waves overflowed the shore, and there was a great roaring under the water, like thunder. By and by Kuksu came up out of the water, but young again, just like a young man. Then Earth-Initiate came and spoke to the people, and said, "If you do as I tell you, everything will be well. When any of you grow old, so old that you cannot walk, come to this lake, or get someone to bring you here. You must then go down into the water as you have seen Kuksu do, and you will come out young again." When he had said this, he went away. He left in the night, and went up above.

All this time food had been easy to get, as Earth-Initiate had wished. The women set out baskets at night, and in the morning they found them full of food, all ready to eat, and lukewarm. One day Coyote came along. He asked the people how they lived, and they told him that all they had to do was to eat and sleep. Coyote replied, "That is no way to do: I can show you something better." Then he told them how he and Earth-Initiate had had a discussion before men had been made; how Earth-Initiate wanted everything easy, and that there should be no sickness or death, but how he had thought it would be better to have people work, get sick, and die. He said, "We'll have a burning." The people did not know what he meant; but Coyote said, "I'll show you. It is better to have a burning, for then the widows can be free." So he took all the baskets and things that the people had, hung them up on poles, made everything all ready. When all was prepared, Coyote said, "At this time you must always have games." So he fixed the moon during which these games were to be played.

Coyote told them to start the games with a foot race, and everyone got ready to run. Kuksu did not come, however. He sat in his hut alone, and was sad, for he knew what was going to occur. Just at this moment Rattlesnake came to Kuksu, and said, "What shall we do now? Everything is spoiled!" Kuksu did not answer, so Rattlesnake said, "Well, I'll do what I think is best." Then he went out, along the course that the racers were to go over, and hid himself, leaving his head just sticking out of a hole. By this time all the racers had started, and among them Coyote's son. He was Coyote's only child, and was very quick. He soon began to outstrip all the runners, and was in the lead. As he passed the spot where Rattlesnake had hidden himself, however, Rattlesnake raised his head and bit the boy in the ankle. In a minute the boy was dead.

Coyote was dancing about the home-stake. He was very happy, and was shouting at his son and praising him. When Rattlesnake bit the boy, and he fell dead, everyone laughed at Coyote, and said, "Your son has fallen down, and is so ashamed that he does not dare to get up." Coyote said, "No, that is not it. He is dead." This was the first death. The people, however, did not understand, and picked the boy up, and brought him to Coyote. Then Coyote began to cry, and everyone did the same. These were the first tears. Then Coyote took his son's body and carried it to the lake of which Earth-Initiate had told them, and threw the body in. But there was no noise, and nothing happened, and the body drifted about for four days on the surface, like a log. On the fifth day Coyote took four sacks of beads and brought them to Kuksu, begging him to restore his son to life. Kuksu did not answer. For five days Coyote begged, then Kuksu came out of his house bringing all his beads and bearskins, and calling to all the people to come and watch him. He laid the body on a bearskin, dressed it, and wrapped it up carefully. Then he dug a grave, put the body into it, and covered it up. Then he told the people, "From now on, this is what you must do. This is the way you must do till the world shall be made over."

About a year after this, in the spring, all was changed. Up to this time everybody spoke the same language. The people were having a burning, everything was ready for the next day, when in the night everybody suddenly began to speak a different language. Each man and his wife, however, spoke the same. Earth-Initiate had come in the night to Kuksu, and had told him about it all, and given him instructions for the next day.

So, when morning came, Kuksu called all the people together, for he was able to speak all the languages. He told them each the names of the different animals, in their languages, taught them how to cook and to hunt, gave them all their laws, and set the time for all their dances and festivals. Then he called each tribe by name, and sent them off in different directions, telling them where they were to live. He sent the warriors to the north, the singers to the west, the flute-players to the east, and the dancers to the south. So all the people went away, and left Kuksu and his wife alone at Tadoiko. By and by his wife went away, leaving in the night, and going first to Estobusin Yamani. Kuksu stayed at Tadoiko a little while longer, and then he also went there, went into the spirit house (*Kukinim Kumi*), and sat down on the south side. He found Coyote's son there, sitting on the north side. The door was on the west.

Coyote had been trying to find out where Kuksu had gone, and where his own son had gone, and at last found the tracks, and followed them to the spirit house. Here he saw Kuksu and his son, the latter eating spirit food (*Kukinim pe*). Coyote wanted to go in, but Kuksu said, "No, wait there. You have just what you wanted, it is your own fault. Every man will now have all kinds of troubles and accidents, will have to work to get his food, and will die and be buried. This must go on till the time is out, and Earth-Initiate come again, and everything will be made over. You must go home, and tell all the people that you have seen your son, that he is not dead." Coyote said he would go, but that he was hungry, and wanted some of the food. Kuksu replied, "You cannot eat that. Only ghosts may eat that food." Then Coyote went away and told all the people, "I saw my son and Kuksu, and he told me to kill myself." So he climbed up to the top of a tall tree, jumped off, and was killed. Then he went to the spirit house, thinking he could now have some of the food; but there was no one there, nothing at all, and so he went out, and walked away to the west, and was never seen again. Kuksu and Coyote's son, however, had gone up above.

Old Man Makes the Land and the People

All animals of the plains at one time heard and knew him, and all birds of the air heard and knew him. All things that he had made understood him, when he spoke to them—the birds, the animals, and the people.

Old Man was traveling about, south of here, making the people. He came from the south, traveling north, making animals and birds as he passed along. He made the mountains, prairies, timber, and brush first. So he went along, traveling northward, making things as he went, putting rivers here and there, and falls on them, putting red paint here and there in the ground, fixing up the world as we see it today. He made the Milk River, the Teton, and crossed it, and being tired, went up on a little hill and lay down to rest.

As he lay on his back, stretched out on the ground, with arms extended, he marked himself out with stones—the shape of his body, head, legs, arms, and everything. There you can see those rocks today. After he had rested, he went on northward, and stumbled over a knoll and fell down on his knees. Then he said, "You are a bad thing to be stumbling against"; so he raised up two large buttes there, and named them the Knees, and they are called so to this day. He went on farther north, and with some of the rocks he carried with him he built the Sweet Grass Hills.

Old Man covered the plains with grass for the animals

to feed on. He marked off a piece of ground, and in it he made to grow all kinds of roots and berries—camas, wild carrots, wild turnips, sweetroot, bitterroot, service berries, bullberries, cherries, plums, and rosebuds. He put trees on the ground. He put all kinds of animals on the ground. When he made the bighorn with its big head and horns, he made it out on the prairie. It did not seem to travel easily on the prairie; it was awkward and could not go fast. So he took it by one of its horns, and led it up into the mountains, and turned it loose; and it skipped about among the rocks, and went up fearful places with ease. So he said, "This is the place that suits you; this is what you are fitted for, the rocks and the mountains." While he was in the mountains, he made the antelope out of dirt, and turned it loose, to see how it would go. It ran so fast that it fell over some rocks and hurt itself. He saw that this would not do, and took the antelope down on the prairie, and turned it loose; and it ran away fast and gracefully, and he said, "This is what you are suited to."

One day Old Man determined that he would make a woman and a child; so he formed them both—the woman and the child, her son—of clay. After he had molded the clay in human shape, he said to the clay, "You must be people," and then he covered it up and left it, and went away. The next morning he went to the place and took the covering off, and saw that the clay shapes had changed a little. The second morning there was still more change, and the third still more. The fourth morning he went to the place, took the covering off, looked at the images, and told them to rise and walk; and they did so. They walked down to the river with their Maker, and then he told them that his name was Napi, Old Man.

As they were standing by the river, the woman said to him, "How is it? Will we always live, will there be no end to it?" He said, "I have never thought of that. We will have to decide it. I will take this buffalo chip and throw it in the river. If it floats, when people die, in four days they will become alive again; they will die for only four days. But if it sinks, there will be an end to them." He threw the chip into the river and it floated. The woman turned and picked up a stone, and said, "No, I will throw this stone in the river; if it floats we will always live, if it sinks people must die, that they may always be sorry for each other." The woman threw the stone into the water, and it sank. "There," said Old Man, "you have chosen. There will be an end to them."

It was not many nights after, that the woman's child died, and she cried a great deal for it. She said to Old Man, "Let us change this. The law that you first made, let that be a law." He said, "Not so. What is made law must be law. We will undo nothing that we have done. The child is dead, but it cannot be changed. People will have to die."

That is how we came to be people. It is he who made us.

The first people were poor and naked, and did not know how to get a living. Old Man showed them the roots and berries, and told them that they could eat them; that in a certain month of the year they could peel the bark off some trees and eat it, that it was good. He told the people that the animals should be their food, and gave them to the people, saying, "These are your herds." He said, "All these little animals that live in the ground—rats, squirrels, skunks, beavers—are good to eat. You need not fear to eat of their flesh." He made all the birds that fly, and told the people that there was no harm in their flesh, that it could be eaten. The first people that he created he used to take about through the timber and swamps and over the prairies, and show them the different plants. Of a certain plant he would say, "The root of this plant, if gathered in a certain month of the year, is good for a certain sickness." So they learned the power of all herbs.

In those days there were buffalo. Now the people had no arms; but those black animals with long beards were armed; and once, as the people were moving about, the buffalo saw them, and ran after them, and hooked them, and killed and ate them. One day, as the Maker of the people was traveling over the country, he saw some of his children, that he had made, lying dead, torn to pieces and partly eaten by the buffalo. When he saw this he was very sad. He said, "This will not do. I will change them. The people shall eat the buffalo."

He went to some of the people who were left, and said to them, "How is it that you people do nothing to these animals that are killing you?" The people said, "What can we do? We have no way to kill these animals, while they are armed and can kill us." Then said the Maker, "That is not hard. I will make you a weapon that will kill these animals." So he went out, and cut some service-berry shoots, and brought them in, and peeled the bark off them. He took a larger piece of wood, and flattened it, and tied a string to it, and made a bow. Now, as he was the master of all birds and could do with them as he wished, he went out and caught one, and took feathers from its wing, and split them, and tied them to the shaft of wood. He tied four feathers along the shaft, and tried the arrow at a mark, and found that it did not fly well. He took these feathers off, and put on three; and when he tried it again, he found that it was good. He went out and began to break sharp pieces off the stones. He tried them, and found that the black flint stones made the best arrow points, and some white flints. Then he taught the people how to use these things.

Then he said, "The next time you go out, take these things with you, and use them as I tell you, and do not run from these animals. When they run at you, as soon as they get pretty close, shoot the arrows at them, as I have taught you; and you will see that they will run from you or will run in a circle around you."

Now, as people became plenty, one day three men went out onto the plain to see the buffalo, but they had no arms. They saw the animals, but when the buffalo saw the men, they ran after them and killed two of them, but one got away. One day after this, the people went on a little hill to look about, and the buffalo saw them, and said, "*Saiyah,* there is some more of our food." And they rushed on the people. This time the people did not run. They began to shoot at the buffalo with the bows and arrows Napi had given them, and the buffalo began to fall; but in the fight a person was killed.

At this time these people had flint knives given them, and they cut up the bodies of the dead buffalo. It is not healthful to eat the meat raw, so Old Man gathered soft dry rotten driftwood and made punk of it, and then got a piece of hardwood, and drilled a hole in it with an arrow point. He gave the people the pointed piece of hardwood, and taught them how to make a fire with fire sticks, and to cook the flesh of these animals and eat it.

They got a kind of stone that was in the land, and then took another harder stone and worked one upon the other, and hollowed out the softer one, and made a kettle of it. This was the fashion of their dishes.

Also Old Man said to the people, "Now, if you are overcome, you may go and sleep, and get power. Something will come to you in your dreams, that will help you. Whatever these animals tell you to do, you must obey them, as they appear to you in your sleep. Be guided by them. If anybody wants help, if you are alone and traveling, and cry aloud for help, your prayer will be answered. It may be by the eagles, perhaps by the buffalo, or by the bears. Whatever animal answers your prayer, you must listen to him."

That was how the first people got through the world, by the power of their dreams.

After this, Old Man kept on, traveling north. Many of the animals that he had made followed him as he went. The animals understood him when he spoke to them, and he used them as his servants. When he got to the north point of the Porcupine Mountains, there he made some more mud images of people, and blew breath upon them, and they became people. He made men and women. They asked him, "What are we to eat?" He made many images of clay in the form of buffalo. Then he blew breath on these, and they stood up; and when he made signs to them, they started to run. Then he said to the people, "Those are your food." They said to him, "Well, now, we have those animals; how are we to kill them?" "I will show you," he said. He took them to a cliff, and made them build two lines of rock piles so that they slanted together toward a small opening at the edge of the cliff. He made the people hide behind these piles of rocks, and said, "When I lead the buffalo this way, as I bring them opposite to you, rise up."

After he had told them how to act, he started on toward a herd of buffalo. He began to call them, and the buffalo started to run toward him, and they followed him until they were inside the lines. Then he dropped back; and as the people rose up, the buffalo ran in a straight line and jumped over the cliff. He told the people to go and take the flesh of those animals. They tried to tear the limbs apart, but they could not. They tried to bite pieces out, and could not.

So Old Man went to the edge of the cliff, and broke some pieces of stone with sharp edges, and told them to cut the flesh with these. When they had taken the skins from these animals, they set up some poles and put the hides on them, and so made a shelter to sleep under. There were some of these buffalo that went over the cliff that were not dead. Their legs were broken, but they were still alive. The people cut strips of green hide, and tied stones in the middle, and made large mauls, and broke in the skulls of the buffalo, and killed them.

After he had taught those people these things, he started off again, traveling north, until he came to where the Bow and Elbow rivers meet. There he made some more people, and taught them the same things. From here he again went on northward. When he had come nearly to the Red Deer's River, he reached the hill where the Old Man sleeps. There he lay down and rested himself. The form of his body is to be seen there yet.

When he awoke from his sleep, he traveled farther northward and came to a fine high hill. He climbed to the top of it, and there sat down to rest. He looked over the country below him, and it pleased him. Before him the hill was steep, and he said to himself, "Well, this is a fine place for sliding; I will have some fun," and he began to slide down the hill. The marks where he slid down are to be seen yet, and the place is known to all people as the Old Man's Sliding Ground.

This is as far as the Blackfeet followed Old Man. The Crees know what he did farther north.

In later times once, Napi said, "Here I will mark you off a piece of ground," and he did so. Then he said: "There is your land, and it is full of all kinds of animals, and many things grow in this land. Let no other people come into it. This is for you five tribes (Blackfeet, Bloods, Piegans, Gros Ventres, Sarcees). When people come to cross the line, take your bows and arrows, your lances and your battle-axes, and give them battle and keep them out. If they gain a footing, trouble will come to you."

Our forefathers gave battle to all people who came to cross these lines, and kept them out. Of late years we have let our friends, the white people, come in, and you know the result. We, his children, have failed to obey his laws.

The Origin of Daylight

Raven flew inland toward the east. He went on for a long time, and finally he was very tired, so he dropped down on the sea the little round stone which his father had given to him. It became a large rock way out at sea. Raven rested on it and refreshed himself, and took off the raven skin.

At that time there was always darkness. There was no daylight then. Again Raven put on the raven skin and flew toward the east. Now, Raven reached the mainland and arrived at the mouth of Skeena River. There he stopped and scattered the salmon roe and trout roe. He said while he was scattering them, "Let every river and creek have all kinds of fish!" Then he took the dried sea-lion bladder and scattered the fruits all over the land, saying, "Let every mountain, hill, valley, plain, the whole land, be full of fruits!"

The whole world was still covered with darkness. When the sky was clear, the people would have a little light from the stars; and when clouds were in the sky, it was very dark all over the land. The people were distressed by this. Then Raven thought that it would be hard for him to obtain his food if it were always dark. He remembered that there was light in heaven, whence he had come. Then he made up his mind to bring down the light to our world. On the following day Raven put on his raven skin, which his father the chief had given to him, and flew upward.

Finally he found the hole in the sky, and he flew through it. Raven reached the inside of the sky. He took off the raven skin and put it down near the hole of the sky. He went on, and came to a spring near the house of the chief of heaven. There he sat down and waited.

Then the chief's daughter came out, carrying a small bucket in which she was about to fetch water. She went down to the big spring in front of her father's house. When Raven saw her coming along, he transformed himself into the leaf of a cedar and floated on the water. The chief's daughter dipped it up in her bucket and drank it. Then she returned to her father's house and entered.

After a short time she was with child, and not long after she gave birth to a boy. Then the chief and his wife were very glad. They washed the boy regularly. He began to grow up. Now he was beginning to creep about. They washed him often, and the chief smoothed and cleaned the floor of the house. Now the child was strong and crept about every day. He began to cry, *"Hama, hama!"* He was crying all the time, and the great chief was troubled, and called in some of his slaves to carry about the boy. The slaves did so, but he would not sleep for several nights. He kept on crying, *"Hama, hama!"* Therefore the chief invited all his wise men, and said to them that he did not know what the boy wanted and why he was crying. He wanted the box that was hanging in the chief's house.

This box, in which the daylight was kept, was hanging in one corner of the house. Its name was *Ma*. Raven had known it before he descended to our world, so the child cried for it. The chief was annoyed, and the wise men listened to what the chief told them. When the wise men heard the child crying aloud, they did not know what he was saying. He was crying all the time, *"Hama, hama, hama!"*

One of the wisest men, who understood him, said to the chief, "He is crying for the *ma*." Therefore the chief ordered it to be taken down. The man put it down. They put it down near the fire, and the boy sat down near it and ceased crying. He stopped crying, for he was glad. Then he rolled the *ma* about inside the house. He did so for four days. Sometimes he would carry it to the door. Now the great chief did not think of it. He had quite forgotten it. Then the boy really took up the *ma,* put it on his shoulders, and ran out with it. While he was running, someone said, "Raven is running away with the *ma!*" He ran away, and the hosts of heaven pursued him. They shouted that Raven was running away with the *ma.* He came to the hole of the sky, put on the skin of the raven, and flew down, carrying the *ma.* Then the hosts of heaven returned to their houses, and he flew down with it to our world.

At that time the world was still dark. He arrived farther up the river, and went down river. Raven had come down near the mouth of Nass River. He went to the mouth of Nass River. It was always dark, and he carried the *ma* about with him. He went on, and went up the river in the dark. A little farther up he heard the noise of the people, who were catching *olachen* in bag nets in their canoes. There was much noise out on the river, because they were working hard.

Raven, who was sitting on the shore, said, "Throw ashore one of the things that you are catching, my dear people!" After a while, Raven said again, "Throw ashore one of the things you are catching!" Then those on the water scolded him. "Where did you come from, great liar, whom they call Raven?" The animal people knew that it was Raven. Therefore they made fun of him. Then Raven said again, "Throw ashore one of the things that you are catching, or I shall break the *ma!*" And all those who were on the water answered, "Where did you get what you are talking about, you liar?" Raven said once more, "Throw ashore one of the things that you are catching, my dear people, or I shall break the *ma* for you!" One person replied, scolding him.

Raven had repeated his request four times, but those

on the water refused what he had asked for. Therefore Raven broke the *ma*. It broke, and it was daylight. The north wind began to blow hard; and all the fishermen, the frogs, were driven away down river until they arrived at one of the large mountainous islands. Here the frogs tried to climb up the rock; but they stuck to the rock, being frozen by the north wind, and became stone. They are still on the rock. The fishing frogs named him Raven, and all the world had the daylight.

The Four Winds

The mighty Master of the Winds of the Earth was sad. His sorrow was not because he was too weak. No. His sadness was caused because he was too strong. His giant strength made him a prisoner of his own power in the Western Sky, though he wished to roam in all directions. When he opened the doors of his Great Blue Wigwam, terrible winds shook the earth far below. He must divide his power, he decided, so that from each door of his great lodge in the sky would blow a separate wind.

He filled his mighty lungs with the loud, biting wind from the North and leaning far out of the North Door of his lodge, blew a bellowing breath to call the creatures of the earth to his aid. When he threw the North Door open, the fierce, whistling winter wind and driving snow which filled the somber sky was too strong and savage for most of the animals that heard the call. They could not fight their way through the storm. The Wind Master only saw some huge, battling shapes moving slowly in the direction of his wigwam. At last, with a great rumbling growl, a mighty, snow-covered bear, which had mastered the biting blast, stood at the door of the lodge.

"You are mighty, O Bear, and your powerful paws can hold my strongest winds in check. You will be the North Wind."

The head of the great beast swayed from side to side as the Master of the Winds took a collar of elk hide and fastened it securely around the animal's neck. With a strong leash he secured the Bear to the North Door of the Great Blue Wigwam.

Opening the massive door on the West side of his lodge, the Wind Master once again drew a deep breath and sent his summoning cry far out over the earth. As the door opened, dark, cold clouds filled the sky. Shrill shrieks and screams rent the air. Fierce fights raged around the lodge. Then, with a screeching snarl, a great green-eyed panther sprang into the doorway. Its eyes blazed like green fire. Its strong, lithe, tawny body quivered, and its long, heavy tail lashed from side to side.

"You are fierce, strong and fearless," praised the Master of the Winds. "You will be the West Wind." With a collar and leash of buffalo hide he bound the Panther to the West Door.

Striding to the eastern side of his lodge, the Master of the Winds flung the East Door wide and sent a piercing call echoing through the sky. At once, icy rain sleeted into the wigwam, and the world was shrouded in a gray mist. A crashing, trampling sound filled the air. The lodge shook. Suddenly a giant moose filled the doorway.

"Welcome, Moose of the misty breath, mighty antlers, and slashing hoofs which cut like a biting wind. You, too, can uproot trees like a storm. I choose you as the East Wind." So saying, the Wind Master took strong, green sinews and tied the Moose to the East Door of the wigwam.

One door still remained—the one on the southern side. The Master of the Winds opened it gently and called softly to the creatures. As the door opened, butterflies fluttered in amidst a shower of multicolored wild flowers. The lodge was filled with their perfume and the soft singing of balmy breezes. Light steps sounded outside and a little, graceful, spotted fawn stood trembling on slender legs at the entrance of the lodge.

"Enter, Little One," invited the Master of the Winds kindly. "You are all softness, beauty, and tenderness. Your step is light as the falling feather from a bird, and your breath sweet as the scent of flowers in the Moon of Roses. You shall be the South Wind." The Master stroked the silky head of the lovely little creature as he lightly wove a colorful collar of fragrant flowers around its slender neck. With a garland of varicolored vines he tenderly attached the dappled Fawn to the South Door of the Great Blue Wigwam, which is the sky.

From that time, when the wind from the North shook the elm-bark covering their lodges, the Iroquois said, "Ho! The Bear growls."

When the wind whimpered from the West, the Iroquois mother told her children, "The Panther whines."

As the hunters on the trail of the deer felt the bite of the wind from the East, they observed, "The Moose breathes hard."

When the soft, serene breeze from the South sang in the pines, the children whispered, "Listen, the Fawn greets her mother."

How the Tribes Began

Many generations ago Aba, the Good Spirit above, created many people, all Choctaw, who spoke the language of the Choctaw. They came from the bosom of the earth, being formed of yellow clay, and no people had ever lived before them. One day all came together and, looking upward, wondered what the clouds and the blue expanse above might be. They talked among themselves, and at last they decided to try to reach the sky.

So they brought many rocks and began building a mound that was to have touched the heavens. That night, however, the wind blew strong from above, and the rocks fell from the mound. The second morning they again began work on the mound, but as the people slept that night, the rocks were again scattered by the winds. Again, on the third morning, the builders went to their task, but as the people were wrapped in slumber that night, the winds came with great force and the rocks were hurled down on them.

The people were not killed, but when daylight came and they began to speak to one another, all were astounded. They spoke various languages and could not understand one another. Some continued to speak the original tongue, and from these sprang the Choctaw tribe. The others began to fight among themselves. Finally they separated. The Choctaw remained the original people. The others scattered and formed various tribes. This explains why there are so many tribes in the land.

The Discovery of Fire

In ancient times when a Mohawk boy had reached the age of fourteen winters, it was customary for him to make a journey, accompanied by his father, to some sacred place up in the mountains. There, after receiving instructions from his father, the youth would remain alone for at least four days. During these four or more days, the Mohawk boy would perform a ceremony known as the Dream Fast. This Dream Fast was very important to the Indian boy of long ago. To be successful in the Dream Fast meant that the Indian was no longer a youth but a man. During the fast, the clan spirit of the young Mohawk would appear to him in a dream and reveal to him the bird, animal, or plant that was to be his guardian throughout his life. After the fast, he must obtain something from the creature of his dream and must wear it in his medicine bag as a charm.

The Mohawk Iroquois had three clans which were, the Bear clan, Turtle clan, and Wolf clan. Should the dreamer belong to the Turtle clan, the spirit of the turtle would appear to him in a dream and show him his future guardian. If the clan spirit did not appear to him during the fast, his father who visited him daily would release him, and he departed home, a failure. He could not have two chances. The dreamer could leave his fasting place after sunset for brief periods. He could drink water to quench his thirst. He was not allowed to eat any food.

Otjiera belonged to the Bear clan and was the son of a

23

famous leader. He had many honors to his credit. No youth of the Mohawks was fleeter on foot than he. He led in the games and was one of the best lacrosse players of his nation. He could shoot his arrow farther and straighter than any of his friends. He knew the forests and streams and would always return from the hunt loaded down with deer meat, which he always divided with the needy of his people. He could imitate the calls of the birds. They would come when he called and would sit on his shoulders. He was the pride of his people.

The time for the Dream Fast of Otjiera had come. It was in the Moon of Strawberries. Otjiera was eager to try the test of strength and endurance. High upon the mountain, on a huge ledge of rock, he built his lodge of young saplings. He covered it with the branches of the balsam to shelter it from the rains. He removed all of his clothing save his breechclout and moccasins. Appealing to his clan spirit, he entered the crude shelter.

Four suns had passed and yet the young warrior had not been visited by the clan spirit. The fifth sun had dawned when his father appeared. He shook the lodge poles and called for Otjiera to come forth. Otjiera in a low and weak voice begged his father to give him one more day. His father left, telling Otjiera that tomorrow he must return to his village.

That night Otjiera looked down from his lodge on the mountains. In the distance he heard low rumblings of thunder. As he listened, the thunder became louder and louder. Bright flashes of lightning lit up the heavens.

"Great Thunder Man, Ra-ti-we-ras," prayed the youth, "send my clan spirit to help me." He had no sooner spoken than a blinding flash of lightning lit the sky and a rumble of thunder shook the mountaintop. Otjiera looked and beheld his clan spirit. A huge bear stood beside him in his lodge. Suddenly the bear spoke, "This night, Otjiera, you shall have a magic that will not only aid you, but will also aid all of the Ongwe-Oweh, the Real People."

There was a blinding flash of lightning, and Otjiera

awoke from his vision. He rubbed his eyes and looked for the clan spirit. The bear was gone. The youth wondered what his guardian helper would be. He looked out from his lodge. The storm had not yet left the mountain. Suddenly he heard a strange sound outside near the lodge. It was a dreadful screeching sound such as he had never heard before. He wondered what kind of animal or bird made such a dreadful noise. The sound had ceased. Then, almost over his head, he saw the cause of the sound. The wind was causing two balsam trees to rub their branches against each other. As the wood rubbed, the friction caused the strange, screeching sound. As Otjiera watched he saw a strange thing happen. The strong wind, rushing up the mountain, caused the trees to bend and sway more rapidly. Where the two trees rubbed against each other, a thin string of smoke appeared. As the boy watched, the wood burst into flame.

Otjiera was frightened at first. He started to run. None of his people had even seen fire so near, and it was feared. The boy remembered his clan spirit. "This must be what the great bear meant," thought the boy.

That day Otjiera took two pieces of dry balsam wood. He rubbed the wood together as he had seen the storm do the night before. He soon tired and was about to throw the wood away when he noticed a thin thread of smoke coming from the wood. He rubbed harder, and soon a tiny spark appeared. By using some dry cedar bark and grass he soon had a fire.

When his father and two chiefs came that noon, they found a happy Otjiera. He had a very powerful helper, a strong medicine which afterward was to help all of his people. That was how fire came to the Indian people of long ago.

The Origin of the Buffalo and of Corn

When the Cheyenne were still in the north, they camped in a large circle. At the entrance of the camp circle, there was a deep spring of water rapidly flowing from out the hillside. They camped near this spring so that they might get their water easily.

One bright day they were playing the game of ring and javelin in the center of the circle. The game consisted of a hoop painted red and black all over, and four throwing sticks which were to be thrown at the hoop when it was rolled. Two of the sticks were painted red, and two were painted black. The sticks were three or four feet long, and were tied together in pairs. The hoop was rolled along the ground, and as it rolled, the red or the black sticks were thrown at it, and the contestants won accordingly as the black or red portion of the ring fell upon the black or red sticks as it stopped. The owner of the stick which matched the color of that portion of the ring that fell on it won.

There was a large crowd of Cheyenne gathered in the middle of the camp, watching the game. As the players contested there came from the south side of the camp circle a certain young man to witness the game. He stood outside of the crowd to look on. He wore a buffalo robe with the hair side turned out, his body was painted yellow, and a yellow-painted eagle breath-feather stuck up on top of his head.

Soon there came from the north side of the camp circle another young man to see the game, and he was dressed exactly like the man who came from the south side. He also stood outside of the crowd, and opposite the first man, to view the game. When they saw each other they went inside the crowd and met face to face and asked each other questions. They were unacquainted with each other, and were surprised when they saw that they were dressed alike.

The crowd stopped playing the game, and stood around to hear what the two young men said. The man from the south said to the man from the north, "My friend, you are imitating my manner of dress. Why do you do it?" Then the man from the north said, "Why do you imitate my manner of dress?" At last each told the other the reason for his manner of dress on that day. Each claimed to have entered the spring that flowed out from the hillside at the entrance to the camp circle, where he had been instructed to dress after this fashion.

They then told the great crowd that they were going to enter the spring again, and that they would soon come out. The crowd watched them as they approached the spring. The man from the south side reached the spring, covered his head with his buffalo robe, and entered. The other young man did the same thing. They splashed the water as they went, and soon found themselves in a large cave.

Near the entrance sat an old woman cooking some buffalo meat and corn in two separate earthen pots. The woman welcomed them thus, "Grandchildren, you have come. I have been expecting you, and am cooking for you. Come and sit down beside me." They sat down, one on each side of her, and told her that their people were hungry, and that they had come to her for their relief. The woman gave them corn from one pot and meat from the other. They ate, and were filled, and when they were through the pots were as full as when they began.

Then the old woman told the young men to look toward

the south. They looked, and they saw the land to the south covered with buffalo. She then told them to look to the west. They looked, and saw all manner of animals, large and small, and there were ponies; but they knew nothing of ponies in those days, for they never had seen any. She then told them to look to the north. They looked to the north, and saw everywhere growing corn.

Then said the old woman to them, "All this that you have seen shall in the future be yours for food. This night I cause the buffalo to be restored to you. When you leave this place, the buffalo shall follow you, and you and your people shall see them coming from this place before sunset. Take in your robes this uncooked corn. Every springtime plant it in low, moist ground, where it will grow. After it matures you will feed upon it. Take also this meat and corn which I have cooked, and when you have returned to your people, ask them all to sit down in the following order, to eat out of these two pots: first, all males, from the youngest to the oldest, with the exception of one orphan boy; second, all females, from the oldest to the youngest, with the exception of one orphan girl. When all are through eating, the contents of the pots are to be eaten by the orphan boy and the orphan girl."

The two young men went out and obeyed the old woman. When they passed out of the spring, they saw that their entire bodies were painted red, and the breath-feathers of their heads were painted red instead of yellow. They went to their people, and they ate as directed of the corn and the meat, and there was enough for all; and the contents of the pots was not diminished until it came time for the two orphan children, who ate all the food.

Toward sunset the people went to their lodges and began watching the spring closely, and in a short time they saw a buffalo jump from the spring. It jumped and played and rolled, and then returned to the spring. In a little while another buffalo jumped out, then another, and another, and finally they came out so fast that the Cheyenne were no longer able to count them. The buffalo continued to come out until dark, and all night and the following day the whole country out in the distance was covered with buffalo. The buffalo scented the great camp, for they left a long, narrow space where the wind went from the camp.

The next day the Cheyenne surrounded the buffalo. Though they were on foot they ran very fast. For a time they had an abundance of buffalo meat. In the springtime they moved their camp to low, swampy land, where they planted the corn they had received from the medicine spring. It grew rapidly, and every grain they planted brought forth strong stalks, and on each stalk grew from two to four ears of corn. The Cheyenne planted corn every year after this.

In the spring, after the planting of their corn, the Cheyenne went on a buffalo hunt. When they had enough meat to dry to last them for a considerable time, they returned to their cornfields.

Mon-daw-min,
or The Origin of Indian Corn

In times past, a poor Indian was living with his wife and children in a beautiful part of the country. He was not only poor, but was not expert in procuring food for his family, and his children were all too young to give him assistance. Although poor, he was a man of a kind and contented disposition. He was always thankful to the Great Spirit for everything he received.

The same disposition was inherited by his eldest son, who had now arrived at the proper age to undertake the ceremony of the *Ke-ig-uish-im-o-win,* a fast to see what kind of spirit would be his guide and guardian through life. Wunzh, for this was his name, had been an obedient boy from his infancy, and was of a pensive, thoughtful, and mild disposition, so that he was beloved by the whole family. As soon as the first indications of spring appeared, they built him the customary little lodge at a retired spot, some distance from their own, where he would not be disturbed during this solemn rite. In the meantime he prepared himself, and immediately went into it, and commenced his fast.

The first few days, he amused himself in the mornings by walking in the woods and over the mountains, examining the early plants and flowers, and in this way prepared himself to enjoy his sleep, and at the same time stored his mind with pleasant ideas for his dreams. While he rambled through the woods, he felt a strong desire to know how the plants, herbs, and berries grew without any aid from man, and why it was that some species were good to eat and others possessed medicinal or poisonous juices. He recalled these thoughts to mind after he became too languid to walk about, and had confined himself strictly to the lodge. He wished he could dream of something that would prove a benefit to his father and family, and to all others.

"True!" he thought, "the Great Spirit made all things, and it is to him that we owe our lives. But could he not make it easier for us to get our food, than by hunting animals and taking fish? I must try to find out this in my visions."

On the third day he became weak and faint, and kept his bed. He fancied, while thus lying, that he saw a handsome young man coming down from the sky and advancing toward him. He was richly and gaily dressed, having on a great many garments of green and yellow colors, but differing in their deeper or lighter shades. He had a plume of waving feathers on his head, and all his motions were graceful.

"I am sent to you, my friend," said the celestial visitor, "by that Great Spirit who made all things in the sky and on the earth. He has seen and knows your motives in fasting. He sees that it is from a kind and benevolent wish to do good to your people, and to procure a benefit for them, and that you do not seek for strength in war or the praise of warriors. I am sent to instruct you, and show you how you can do your kindred good." He then told the young man to arise, and prepare to wrestle with him, as it was only by this means that he could hope to succeed in his wishes.

Wunzh knew he was weak from fasting, but he felt his courage rising in his heart, and immediately got up, determined to die rather than fail. He commenced the trial, and after a protracted effort, was almost exhausted, when the beautiful stranger said, "My friend, it is enough for once; I will come again to try you"; and smiling on him, he ascended in the air in the same direction from which he came.

The next day the celestial visitor reappeared at the same hour and renewed the trial. Wunzh felt that his strength was even less than the day before, but the courage of his mind seemed to increase in proportion as his body became weaker. Seeing this, the stranger again spoke to him in the same words he used before, adding, "Tomorrow will be your last trial. Be strong, my friend, for this is the only way you can overcome me, and obtain the boon you seek."

On the third day he again appeared at the same time and renewed the struggle. The poor youth was very faint in body, but grew stronger in mind at every contest, and was determined to prevail or perish in the attempt. He exerted his utmost powers, and after the contest had been continued the usual time, the stranger ceased his efforts and declared himself conquered. For the first time he entered the lodge, and sitting down beside the youth, he began to deliver his instructions to him, telling him in what manner he should proceed to take advantage of his victory.

"You have won your desires of the Great Spirit," said the stranger. "You have wrestled manfully. Tomorrow will be the seventh day of your fasting. Your father will give you food to strengthen you, and as it is the last day of trial, you will prevail. I know this, and now tell you what you must do to benefit your family and your tribe. Tomorrow," he repeated, "I shall meet you and wrestle with you for the last time; and as soon as you have prevailed against me, you will strip off my garments and throw me down, clean the earth of roots and weeds, make it soft, and bury me in the spot. When you have done this, leave my body in the earth, and do not disturb it, but come occasionally to visit the place to see whether I have come to life, and be careful never to let the grass or weeds grow on my grave. Once a month cover me with fresh earth. If you follow my instructions, you will accomplish your object of doing good to your fellow creatures by teaching them the knowledge I now teach you." He then shook him by the hand and disappeared.

In the morning the youth's father came with some light refreshments, saying, "My son, you have fasted long enough. If the Great Spirit will favor you, he will do it now. It is seven days since you have tasted food, and you must not sacrifice your life. The Master of Life does not require that."

"My father," replied the youth, "wait till the sun goes down. I have a particular reason for extending my fast to that hour."

"Very well," said the old man, "I shall wait till the hour arrives, and you feel inclined to eat."

At the usual hour of the day, the sky visitor returned, and the trial of strength was renewed. Although the youth had not availed himself of his father's offer of food, he felt that new strength had been given to him, and that exertion had renewed his strength and fortified his courage. He grasped his angelic antagonist with supernatural strength, threw him down, took from him his beautiful garments and plume, and finding him dead, immediately buried him on the spot, taking all the precautions he had been told of, and being very confident, at the same time, that his friend would again come to life.

He then returned to his father's lodge, and partook sparingly of the meal that had been prepared for him. But he never for a moment forgot the grave of his friend. He carefully visited it throughout the spring, and weeded out the grass, and kept the ground in a soft and pliant state. Very soon he saw the tops of the green plumes coming through the ground; and the more careful he was to obey his instructions in keeping the ground in order, the faster they grew. He was, however, careful to conceal the exploit from his father. Days and weeks had passed in this way.

The summer was now drawing toward a close, when one day, after a long absence in hunting, Wunzh invited his father to follow him to the quiet and lonesome spot of his former fast. The lodge had been removed, and the weeds kept from growing on the circle where it stood, but in its place stood a tall and graceful plant, with bright-colored silken hair, surmounted with nodding plumes and stately leaves, and golden clusters on each side.

"It is my friend," shouted the lad; "it is the friend of all mankind. It is *Mon-daw-min.* We need no longer rely on hunting alone; for as long as this gift of corn is cherished and taken care of, the ground itself will give us a living." He then pulled an ear. "See, my father," said he, "this is what I fasted for. The Great Spirit has listened to my voice, and sent us something new, and henceforth our people will not alone depend upon the chase or upon the waters."

He then told his father the instructions given him by the stranger. He told him that the broad husks must be torn away, as he had pulled off the garments in his wrestling. And having done this, directed him how the ear must be held before the fire till the outer skin became brown, while all the milk was retained in the grain. The whole family then united in a feast on the newly grown ears, expressing gratitude to the Merciful Spirit who gave it. So corn came into the world.

The Origin of Wampum

A man walking in a forest saw an unusually large bird covered with a heavily clustered coating of wampum, *oh-ko-ah*. He immediately informed his people and chiefs, whereupon the head chief offered as a prize his beautiful daughter to one who would capture the bird, dead or alive, which apparently had come from another world. Whereupon the warriors, with bows and arrows, went to the "tree of promise," and as each lucky one barely hit the bird it would throw off a large quantity of the coveted coating, which multiplied by being cropped.

At last, when the warriors were despairing of success, a little boy from a neighboring tribe came to satisfy his curiosity by seeing the wonderful bird of which he had heard. But as his people were at war with this tribe he was not permitted by the warriors to try his skill at archery, and was even threatened with death. But the head chief said, "He is a mere boy; let him shoot on equal terms with you who are brave and fearless warriors." His decision being final, the boy, with unequaled skill, brought the coveted bird to the ground.

Having received the daughter of the head chief in marriage, he divided the *oh-ko-ah* between his own tribe and that into which he had married, and peace was declared between them. Then the boy husband decreed that wampum should be the price of peace and blood, which was adopted by all nations. Hence arose the custom of giving belts of wampum to satisfy violated honor, hospitality, or national privilege.

The Origin of the Medicine Pipe

Thunder—you have heard him. He is everywhere. He roars in the mountains, he shouts far out on the prairie. He strikes the high rocks, and they fall to pieces. He hits a tree, and it is broken in slivers. He strikes the people, and they die. He is bad. He does not like the towering cliff, the standing tree, or living man. He likes to strike and crush them to the ground. Yes! yes! Of all he is most powerful; he is the one most strong. But I have not told you the worst: he sometimes steals women.

Long ago, almost in the beginning, a man and his wife were sitting in their lodge, when Thunder came and struck them. The man was not killed. At first he was as if dead, but after a while he lived again, and rising looked about him. His wife was not there. "Oh, well," he thought, "she has gone to get some water or wood," and he sat awhile; but when the sun had underdisappeared, he went out and inquired about her of the people. No one had seen her. He searched throughout the camp, but did not find her. Then he knew that Thunder had stolen her, and he went out on the hills alone and mourned.

When morning came, he rose and wandered far away, and he asked all the animals he met if they knew where Thunder lived. They laughed, and would not answer. The Wolf said, "Do you think we would seek the home of the only one we fear? He is our only danger. From all others we can run away, but from him there is no running. He strikes, and there we lie. Turn back! Go home! Do not look for the dwelling place of that dreadful one." But the man kept on, and traveled far away. Now he came to a lodge, a queer lodge, for it was made of stone—just like any other lodge, only it was made of stone. Here lived the Raven chief. The man entered.

"Welcome, my friend," said the chief of the Ravens. "Sit down, sit down." And food was placed before him.

Then, when he had finished eating, the Raven said, "Why have you come?"

"Thunder has stolen my wife," replied the man. "I seek his dwelling place that I may find her."

"Would you dare enter the lodge of that dreadful person?" asked the Raven. "He lives close by here. His lodge is of stone, like this; and hanging there, within, are eyes, the eyes of those he has killed or stolen. He has taken out their eyes and hung them in his lodge. Now, then, dare you enter there?"

"No," replied the man, "I am afraid. What man could look at such dreadful things and live?"

"No person can," said the Raven. "There is but one old Thunder fears. There is but one he cannot kill. It is I, it is the Raven. Now I will give you medicine, and he shall not harm you. You shall enter there, and seek among those eyes your wife's; and if you find them, tell that Thunder why you came, and make him give them to you. Here, now, is a raven's wing. Just point it at him, and he will start back quick; but if that fails, take this. It is an arrow, and the shaft is made of elk horn. Take this, I say, and shoot it through the lodge."

"Why make a fool of me?" the poor man asked. "My heart is sad. I am crying." And he covered his head with his robe, and wept.

"Oh," said the Raven, "you do not believe me. Come out, come out, and I will make you believe." When they stood outside, the Raven asked, "Is the home of your people far?"

"A great distance," said the man.

"Can you tell how many days you have traveled?"

"No," he replied, "my heart is sad. I did not count the days. The berries have grown and ripened since I left."

"Can you see your camp from here?" asked the Raven.

The man did not speak. Then the Raven rubbed some medicine on his eyes and said, "Look!" The man looked, and saw the camp. It was close. He saw the people. He saw the smoke rising from the lodges.

"Now you will believe," said the Raven. "Take now the arrow and the wing, and go and get your wife."

So the man took these things, and went to the Thunder's lodge. He entered and sat down by the doorway. The Thunder sat within and looked at him with awful eyes. But the man looked above, and saw many pairs of eyes. Among them were those of his wife.

"Why have you come?" said the Thunder in a fearful voice.

"I seek my wife," the man replied, "whom you have stolen. There hang her eyes."

"No man can enter my lodge and live," said the Thunder; and he rose to strike him. Then the man pointed the raven wing at the Thunder, and he fell back on his couch and shivered. But he soon recovered, and rose again. Then the man fitted the elk-horn arrow to his bow, and shot it through the lodge of rock; right through that lodge of rock it pierced a jagged hole, and let the sunlight in.

"Hold," said the Thunder. "Stop; you are the stronger. Yours the great medicine. You shall have your wife. Take down her eyes." Then the man cut the string that held them, and immediately his wife stood beside him.

"Now," said the Thunder, "you know me. I am of great power. I live here in summer, but when winter comes, I go far south. I go south with the birds. Here is my pipe. It is medicine. Take it, and keep it. Now, when I first come in the spring, you shall fill and light this pipe, and you shall pray to me, you and the people. For I bring the rain which makes the berries large and ripe. I bring the rain which makes all things grow, and for this you shall pray to me, you and all the people."

Thus the people got the first medicine pipe. It was long ago.

Scarface, or The Origin of
the Medicine Lodge

In the earliest times there was no war. All the tribes were at peace. In those days there was a man who had a daughter, a very beautiful girl. Many young men wanted to marry her, but every time she was asked, she only shook her head and said she did not a want a husband.

"How is this?" asked her father. "Some of these young men are rich, handsome, and brave."

"Why should I marry?" replied the girl. "I have a rich father and mother. Our lodge is good. The parfleches are never empty. There are plenty of tanned robes and soft furs for winter. Why worry me, then?"

The Raven Bearers held a dance; they all dressed carefully and wore their ornaments, and each one tried to dance the best. Afterward some of them asked for this girl, but still she said no. Then the Bulls, the Kit-foxes, and others of the *I-kun-uh-kah-tsi* held their dances, and all those who were rich, many great warriors, asked this man for his daughter, but to every one of them she said no. Then her father was angry, and said, "Why, now, this way? All the best men have asked for you, and still you say no. I believe you have a secret lover."

"Ah!" said her mother. "What shame for us should a child be born and our daughter still unmarried!" "Father! mother!" replied the girl, "pity me. I have no secret lover, but now hear the truth. That Above Person, the Sun, told

39

me, 'Do not marry any of those men, for you are mine; thus you shall be happy, and live to great age'; and again he said, 'Take heed. You must not marry. You are mine.'"

"Ah!" replied the father. "It must always be as he says." And they talked no more about it.

There was a poor young man, very poor. His father, mother, all his relations, had gone to the Sand Hills. He had no lodge, no wife to tan his robes or sew his moccasins. He stopped in one lodge today, and tomorrow he ate and slept in another; thus he lived. He was a good-looking young man, except that on his cheek he had a scar, and his clothes were always old and poor.

After those dances, some of the young men met this poor Scarface, and they laughed at him, and said, "Why don't you ask that girl to marry you? You are so rich and handsome!" Scarface did not laugh; he replied, "Ah! I will do as you say. I will go and ask her." All the young men thought this was funny. They laughed a great deal. But Scarface went down by the river. He waited by the river, where the women came to get water, and by and by the girl came along. "Girl," he said, "wait. I want to speak with you. Not as a designing person do I ask you, but openly where the Sun looks down, and all may see."

"Speak then," said the girl.

"I have seen the days," continued the young man. "You have refused those who are young, and rich, and brave. Now, today, they laughed and said to me, 'Why do you not ask her?' I am poor, very poor. I have no lodge, no food, no clothes, no robes, and warm furs. I have no relations; all have gone to the Sand Hills; yet now, today, I ask you, take pity, be my wife."

The girl hid her face in her robe and brushed the ground with the point of her moccasin, back and forth, back and forth, for she was thinking. After a time she said, "True. I have refused all those rich young men, yet now the poor one asks me, and I am glad. I will be your wife, and my people will be happy. You are poor, but it does not matter. My father will give you dogs. My mother will make us a lodge. My people will give us robes and furs. You will be poor no longer."

Then the young man was happy, and he started to kiss her, but she held him back, and said, "Wait! The Sun has spoken to me. He says I may not marry, that I belong to him. He says if I listen to him, I shall live to great age. But now I say, 'Go to the Sun.' Tell him, 'She whom you spoke with heeds your words. She has never done wrong, but now she wants to marry. I want her for my wife.' Ask him to take that scar from your face. That will be his sign. I will know he is pleased. But if he refuses, or if you fail to find his lodge, then do not return to me."

"Oh!" cried the young man, "at first your words were good. I was glad. But now it is dark. My heart is dead. Where is that far-off lodge? Where the trail, which no one yet has traveled?"

"Take courage, take courage!" said the girl, and she went to her lodge.

Scarface was very sad. He sat down and covered his head with his robe and tried to think what to do. After a while he got up, and went to an old woman who had been kind to him. "Pity me," he said. "I am very poor. I am going away now on a long journey. Make me some moccasins."

"Where are you going?" asked the old woman. "There is no war; we are very peaceful here."

"I do not know where I shall go," replied Scarface. "I am in trouble, but I cannot tell you now what it is."

So the old woman made him some moccasins, seven pairs, with parfleche soles, and also she gave him a sack of food—pemmican of berries, pounded meat, and dried back fat—for this old woman had a good heart. She liked the young man.

All alone, and with a sad heart, he climbed the bluffs and stopped to take a last look at the camp. He wondered if he would ever see his sweetheart and the people again. "*Hai-yu!* Pit me, O Sun," he prayed, and turning, he started to find the trail.

For many days he traveled on, over great prairies, along

timbered rivers and among the mountains, and every day his sack of food grew lighter; but he saved it as much as he could, and ate berries, and roots, and sometimes he killed an animal of some kind. One night he stopped by the home of a wolf. *"Hai-yah!"* said that one, "what is my brother doing so far from home?"

"Ah!" replied Scarface, "I seek the place where the Sun lives; I am sent to speak with him."

"I have traveled far," said the wolf. "I know all the prairies, the valleys, and the mountains, but I have never seen the Sun's home. Wait; I know one who is very wise. Ask the bear. He may tell you."

The next day the man traveled on again, stopping now and then to pick a few berries, and when night came he arrived at the bear's lodge.

"Where is your home?" asked the bear. "Why are you traveling alone, my brother?"

"Help me! Pity me!" replied the young man; "because of her words I seek the Sun. I go to ask him for her."

"I know not where he stops," replied the bear. "I have traveled by many rivers, and I know the mountains, yet I have never seen his lodge. There is someone beyond, that striped-face, who is very smart. Go and ask him."

The badger was in his hole. Stooping over, the young man shouted, "Oh, cunning striped-face! Oh, generous animal! I wish to speak with you."

"What do you want?" said the badger, poking his head out of the hole.

"I want to find the Sun's home," replied Scarface. "I want to speak with him."

"I do not know where he lives," replied the badger. "I never travel very far. Over there in the timber is a wolverine. He is always traveling around, and is of much knowledge. Maybe he can tell you."

Then Scarface went to the woods and looked all around for the wolverine, but could not find him. So he sat down to rest. *"Hai-yu! Hai-yu!"* he cried. "Wolverine, take pity on me. My food is gone, my moccasins worn out. Now I must die."

"What is it, my brother?" he heard, and looking around, he saw the animal sitting near.

"She whom I would marry," said Scarface, "belongs to the Sun; I am trying to find where he lives, to ask him for her."

"Ah!" said the wolverine. "I know where he lives. Wait; it is nearly night. Tomorrow I will show you the trail to the big water. He lives on the other side of it."

Early in the morning, the wolverine showed him the trail, and Scarface followed it until he came to the water's edge. He looked out over it, and his heart almost stopped. Never before had anyone seen such a big water. The other side could not be seen, and there was no end to it. Scarface sat down on the shore. His food was all gone, his moccasins worn out. His heart was sick. "I cannot cross this big water," he said. "I cannot return to the people. Here, by this water, I shall die."

Not so. His helpers were there. Two swans came swimming up to the shore. "Why have you come here?" they asked him. "What are you doing? It is very far to the place where your people live."

"I am here," replied Scarface, "to die. Far away, in my country, is a beautiful girl. I want to marry her, but she belongs to the Sun. So I started to find him and ask for her. I have traveled many days. My food is gone. I cannot go back. I cannot cross this big water, so I am going to die."

"No," said the swans; "it shall not be so. Across this water is the home of that Above Person. Get on our backs, and we will take you there."

Scarface quickly rose. He felt strong again. He waded out into the water and lay down on the swans' backs, and they started off. Very deep and black is that fearful water. Strange people live there, mighty animals which often seize and drown a person. The swans carried him safely, and took him to the other side. Here was a broad hard trail leading back from the water's edge.

"*Kyi,*" said the swans. "You are now close to the Sun's lodge. Follow that trail, and you will soon see it."

Scarface started up the trail, and pretty soon he came to some beautiful things, lying in it. There was a war shirt, a shield, and a bow and arrows. He had never seen such pretty weapons; but he did not touch them. He walked carefully around them, and traveled on. A little way farther on, he met a young man, the handsomest person he had ever seen. His hair was very long, and he wore clothing made of strange skins. His moccasins were sewed with bright colored feathers. The young man said to him, "Did you see some weapons lying on the trail?"

"Yes," replied Scarface, "I saw them."

"But did you not touch them?" asked the young man.

"No, I thought someone had left them there, so I did not take them."

"You are not a thief," said the young man. "What is your name?"

"Scarface."

"Where are you going?"

"To the Sun."

"My name," said the young man, "is A-pi-su-ahts, Morning Star. The Sun is my father; come, I will take you to our lodge. My father is not now at home, but he will come in at night."

Soon they came to the lodge. It was very large and handsome; strange medicine animals were painted on it. Behind, on a tripod, were strange weapons and beautiful clothes—the Sun's. Scarface was ashamed to go in, but Morning Star said, "Do not be afraid, my friend; we are glad you have come."

They entered. One person was sitting there, Ko-ko-mik-e-is, the Moon, the Sun's wife, Morning Star's mother. She spoke to Scarface kindly, and gave him something to eat. "Why have you come so far from your people?" she asked.

Then Scarface told her about the beautiful girl he wanted to marry. "She belongs to the Sun," he said. "I have come to ask him for her."

When it was time for the Sun to come home, the Moon

hid Scarface under a pile of robes. As soon as the Sun got to the doorway, he stopped and said, "I smell a person."

"Yes, father," said Morning Star, "a good young man has come to see you. I know he is good, for he found some of my things on the trail and did not touch them."

Then Scarface came out from under the robes, and the Sun entered and sat down. "I am glad you have come to our lodge," he said. "Stay with us as long as you think best. My son is lonesome sometimes; be his friend."

The next day the Moon called Scarface out of the lodge, and said to him, "Go with Morning Star where you please, but never hunt near that big water; do not let him go there. It is the home of the great birds which have long sharp bills; they kill people. I have had many sons, but these birds have killed them all. Morning Star is the only one left."

So Scarface stayed there a long time and hunted with Morning Star. One day they came near the water, and saw the big birds.

"Come," said Morning Star, "let us go and kill those birds."

"No, no!" replied Scarface; "we must not go there. Those are very terrible birds; they will kill us."

Morning Star would not listen. He ran toward the water, and Scarface followed. He knew that he must kill the birds and save the boy. If not, the Sun would be angry and might kill him. He ran ahead and met the birds, which were coming toward him to fight, and killed every one of them with his spear: not one was left. Then the young men cut off their heads, and carried them home. Morning Star's mother was glad when they told her what they had done, and showed her the birds' heads. She cried, and called Scarface "my son." When the Sun came home at night, she told him about it, and he too was glad. "My son," he said to Scarface, "I will not forget what you have this day done for me. Tell me now, what can I do for you?"

"*Hai-yu,*" replied Scarface. "*Hai-yu,* pity me. I am here to ask you for that girl. I want to marry her. I asked her, and she was glad; but she says you own her, that you told her not to marry."

"What you say is true," said the Sun. "I have watched the days, so I know it. Now, then, I give her to you; she is yours. I am glad she has been wise. I know she has never done wrong. The Sun pities good women. They shall live a long time. So shall their husbands and children. Now you will soon go home. Let me tell you something. Be wise and listen: I am the only chief. Everything is mine. I made the earth, the mountains, prairies, rivers, and forests. I made the people and all the animals. This is why I say I alone am the chief. I can never die. True, the winter makes me old and weak, but every summer I grow young again."

Then said the Sun, "What one of all animals is smartest? The raven is, for he always finds food. He is never hungry. Which one of all the animals is most sacred? The buffalo is. Of all animals, I like him best. He is for the people. He is your food and your shelter. What part of his body is sacred? The tongue is. That is mine. What else is sacred? Berries are. They are mine too. Come with me and see the world." He took Scarface to the edge of the sky, and they looked down and saw it. It is round and flat, and all around the edge is the jumping-off place.

Then said the Sun, "When any man is sick or in danger, his wife may promise to build me a lodge, if he recovers. If the woman is pure and true, then I will be pleased and help the man. But if she is bad, if she lies, then I will be angry. You shall build the lodge like the world, round, with walls, but first you must build a sweat lodge of a hundred sticks. It shall be like the sky, and half of it shall be painted red. That is me. The other half you will paint black. That is the night."

Further said the Sun, "Which is the best, the heart or the brain? The brain is. The heart often lies, the brain never." Then he told Scarface everything about making the medicine lodge, and when he had finished, he rubbed a powerful medicine on his face, and the scar disappeared.

Then he gave him two raven feathers, saying, "These are the sign for the girl that I give her to you. They must always be worn by the husband of the woman who builds a medicine lodge."

The young man was now ready to return home. Morning Star and the Sun gave him many beautiful presents. The Moon cried and kissed him, and called him "my son." Then the Sun showed him the short trail. It was the Wolf Road, the Milky Way. He followed it, and soon reached the ground.

It was a very hot day. All the lodge skins were raised, and the people sat in the shade. There was a chief, a very generous man, and all day long people kept coming to his lodge to feast and smoke with him. Early in the morning this chief saw a person sitting out on a butte near by, close wrapped in his robe. The chief's friends came and went, the sun reached the middle, and passed on, down toward the mountains. Still this person did not move. When it was almost night, the chief cried, "Why does that person sit there so long? The heat has been strong, but he has never eaten nor drunk. He may be a stranger; go and ask him in."

So some young men went up to him, and said, "Why do you sit here in the great heat all day? Come to the shade of the lodges. The chief asks you to feast with him."

Then the person arose and threw off his robe, and they were surprised. He wore beautiful clothes. His bow, shield, and other weapons were of strange make. But they knew his face, although the scar was gone, and they ran ahead, shouting, "The scarface poor young man has come. He is poor no longer. The scar on his face is gone."

All the people rushed out to see him. "Where have you been?" they asked. "Where did you get all these pretty things?" He did not answer. There in the crowd stood that young woman; and taking the two raven feathers from his head, he gave them to her, and said, "The trail was very long, and I nearly died, but by those helpers, I found his lodge. He is glad. He sends these feathers to you. They are the sign."

Great was her gladness then. They were married, and made the first medicine lodge, as the Sun had said. The Sun was glad. He gave them great age. They were never sick. When they were very old, one morning, their children said, "Awake! Rise and eat." They did not move. In the night, in sleep, without pain, their shadows had departed for the Sand Hills.

The First False Face

The powerful Spirit Medicine Man of the Seneca was making magic. All the night before he had led the All Night Medicine Singing, but he was not tired. He stood in a lovely valley which nestled in the mountains. This Medicine Man had suffered much to gain his great skill. He knew all of the magic rites and had even attended the Dark Dance Feast of the Little People. Spirit Medicine Man truly loved people, birds, and animals. For that the Great Good Spirit had granted him vast power.

On this day, Spirit Medicine Man had wonderful power. He made bright flowers flutter from their stems and join the breeze-borne butterflies. When a daring butterfly declared that flowers should not fly, the Medicine Man changed that gleaming jewel of the air into a brilliant flower. The sunflowers begged to see a star, although the sun still rode high in the serene sky. The Medicine Man raised his hand high to the east and west and begged the Great Spirit to grant the wish of the sunflowers. Almost immediately a great star shone brightly in the cloudless sky above the valley and, for the first time, the faces of the sunflowers turned from the sun to a star.

The heart of the Medicine Man was glad that day, and the birds and beasts came close to him to be caressed. Suddenly alarm spread among the wild things. They swiftly left their friend and hid in the trees and bushes. A stranger was coming across the valley toward them. The

Spirit Medicine Man was sorry to be disturbed. He wished to be far from mankind just then and had come to this hidden valley to seek solitude. Still, he greeted the stranger courteously, hoping that he would continue on his way. This was not to be.

"O mighty Spirit Medicine Man, I have traveled for many moons to greet you," said the stranger. "From the wise ones of the plains and hills I have learned much magic. At last I knew all that they could teach me. Then they told me that among the woodland people I would find a maker of magic more powerful far than they. He whom they spoke of was you. So come I to try my magic against yours. You will find that I too have great power," the stranger added boastfully.

Spirit Medicine Man disliked boasting. Still, he believed that the stranger must have considerable skill or he would not have asked for the chance to test it. Well, he would soon see how powerful the magic of the stranger really was. Perhaps in such a test of power he would learn things which he did not now know. Despite his great knowledge, Spirit Medicine Man was humble and always willing to learn.

"Friend, I did not come to this peaceful valley to try my skill against yours nor that of any other medicine man. As you have come, let us make tests for the time it takes the sun to travel the width of a lodge pole, that you may leave with a happy heart. What, O stranger, will you have the test be?"

"Let us try to move one of these mountains," suggested the stranger calmly.

Spirit Medicine Man smiled in surprise. "You would start at the top and reach the bottom of magic-making last!" he exclaimed.

"All other tests will be too simple for magicians such as we," asserted the stranger. As he spoke, he crooked his right forefinger, and two fully grown red foxes ran from their den beneath a great boulder. One climbed onto his right shoulder and the other onto his left. "Such a small test is easy for a maker of magic such as I," boasted the stranger. "This medicine I do not make often because their tails tickle my nose," he confided.

"The wild things must love you well to come so close," remarked Spirit Medicine Man.

"They never leave me until they have my permission to go," replied the stranger.

Spirit Medicine Man moved a pace toward the stranger and crooked his left forefinger. Instantly the two foxes sprang from the shoulders of the stranger and landed on his own.

"Go!" commanded Spirit Medicine Man as the foxes sat motionless on his shoulders. "Your tails tickle my nose."

Silent as shadows, the foxes leaped to the ground and raced to their den.

"Is it still your wish to move a mountain?" inquired Spirit Medicine Man.

"I would like to try," replied the stranger, but his voice was no longer boastful.

"Try first," suggested Spirit Medicine Man, pointing to the mountain that was closest to them. "First let us turn our backs to the mountain as we make our magic. It is good medicine to do so."

They turned their faces from the peak, and the stranger stretched his arms out in front of him, hands open, palms up. "Come to me, mountain!" he commanded.

After a moment the medicine men turned to look at it. The mountain had moved slightly, of that both men felt sure. Loosened rocks were still rolling down its sides from the movement.

"Try once more," advised Spirit Medicine Man kindly. "Your medicine is powerful. You lack only complete faith, not skill."

"After you have made the test I will try again," promised the stranger. He was trembling violently and sweat poured down his face.

Again they turned their backs to the mountain.

High above his head went the arms of Spirit Medicine

Man. A serene smile hovered on his lips. "Come!" he ordered gently.

Instantly there was a mighty rumbling. The earth trembled and shook close to his feet. Spirit Medicine Man was calm and did not move. The stranger swung sharply around. His face struck the side of the mountain with a sickening thud, because the mountain now stood directly behind him. The boastful stranger had learned a hard lesson. His face and mouth were terribly twisted, and his nose was broken and hung to one side. From then on he was called Old Broken Nose.

Spirit Medicine Man took pity on the injured stranger, and when his wounds were healed, taught him how to care for sick people and to cure illness, but Old Broken Nose's face always remained twisted to one side.

Soon the strange, distorted face became a sign of healing, as Old Broken Nose often cured very sick people by blowing hot ashes over them with his twisted mouth. The women of the tribe made little masks resembling the face of the healer and used them as charms and the Dance of the False Faces was started in his honor.

Iosco, or The Prairie Boys' Visit to the Sun and Moon

One pleasant morning, five young men and a boy about ten years of age, called Iosco, went out a-shooting with their bows and arrows. They left their lodges with the first appearance of daylight, and having passed through a long reach of woods, had ascended a high hill before the sun arose. While standing there in a group, the sun suddenly burst forth in all its glory. The air was so clear that it appeared to be at no great distance. "How very near it is," they all said. "It cannot be far," said the eldest, "and if you will accompany me, we will see if we cannot reach it." A loud assent burst from every lip. Even the boy, Iosco, said he would go. They told him he was too young, but he replied, "If you do not permit me to go with you, I will tell your plan to each of your parents." They then said to him, "You shall also go with us, so be quiet."

They then fell upon the following arrangement. It was resolved that each one should obtain from his parents as many pairs of moccasins as he could, and also new clothing of leather. They fixed on a spot where they would conceal all their articles, until they were ready to start on their journey, and which would serve, in the meantime, as a place of rendezvous, where they might secretly meet and consult. This being arranged, they returned home.

A long time passed before they could put their plan into execution. But they kept it a profound secret, even to the

53

boy. They frequently met at the appointed place, and discussed the subject. At length everything was in readiness, and they decided on a day to set out. That morning the boy shed tears for a pair of new leather leggings. "Don't you see," said he to his parents, "how my companions are dressed?" This appeal to their pride and envy prevailed. He obtained the leggings.

Artifices were also resorted to by the others, under the plea of going out on a special hunt. They said to one another, but in a tone that they might be overheard, "We will see who will bring in the most game." They went out in different directions, but soon met at the appointed place, where they had hid the articles for their journey, with as many arrows as they had time to make. Each one took something on his back, and they began their march.

They traveled day after day, through a thick forest, but the sun was always at the same distance. "We must," said they, "travel toward *Waubunong,* the east, and we shall get to the object, some time or other." No one was discouraged, although winter overtook them. They built a lodge and hunted till they obtained as much dried meat as they could carry, and then continued on. This they did several times; season followed season. More than one winter overtook them. Yet none of them became discouraged, or expressed dissatisfaction.

One day the travelers came to the banks of a river, whose waters ran toward the east. They followed it down many days. As they were walking one day, they came to rising ground, from which they saw something white or clear through the trees. They encamped on this elevation. Next morning they came, suddenly, in view of an immense body of water. No land could be seen as far as the eye could reach. One or two of them lay down on the beach to drink. As soon as they got the water in their mouths, they spit it out, and exclaimed, with surprise, *"Shewetagon awbo!"*—salt water. It was the sea.

While looking on the water, the sun arose as if from the deep, and went on its steady course through the heavens, enlivening the scene with his cheering and animating beams. They stood in admiration, but the object appeared to be as distant from them as ever. They thought it best to encamp, and consult whether it were advisable to go on, or return. "We see," said the leader, "that the sun is still on the opposite side of this great water, but let us not be disheartened. We can walk around the shore." To this they all assented.

Next morning they took the northerly shore, to walk around it, but had only gone a short distance when they came to a large river. They again encamped, and while sitting before the fire, the question was put, whether anyone of them had ever dreamed of water, or of walking on it. After a long silence, the eldest said he had. Soon after, they lay down to sleep.

When they arose the following morning, the eldest addressed them: "We have done wrong in coming north. Last night my spirit appeared to me, and told me to go south, and that but a short distance beyond the spot we left yesterday, we should come to a river with high banks. That by looking off its mouth, we should see an island, which would approach to us. He directed that we should all get on it. He then told me to cast my eyes toward the water. I did so, and I saw all he had declared. He then informed me that we must return south, and wait at the river until the day after tomorrow. I believe all that was revealed to me in this dream, and that we shall do well to follow it."

The party immediately retraced their footsteps in exact obedience to this dream. Toward the evening they came to the borders of the indicated river. It had high banks, behind which they encamped, and here they patiently awaited the fulfillment of the dream. The appointed day arrived. They said, "We will see if that which has been said will be seen. Midday is the promised time." Early in the morning two had gone to the shore to keep a lookout. They waited anxiously for the middle of the day, straining their eyes to see if they could discover anything.

Suddenly they raised a shout, "*Ewaddee suh neen!*—There it is! There it is!"

On rushing to the spot they beheld something like an island steadily advancing toward the shore. As it approached, they could discover that something was moving on it in various directions. They said, "It is a Manito, let us be off into the woods." "No, no," cried the eldest, "let us stay and watch." It now became stationary, and lost much of its imagined height. They could only see three trees, as they thought, resembling trees in a pinery that had been burned. The wind, which had been off the sea, now died away into a perfect calm. They saw something leaving the fancied island and approaching the shore, throwing and flapping its wings, like a loon when he attempts to fly in calm weather. It entered the mouth of the river.

They were on the point of running away, but the eldest dissuaded them. "Let us hide in this hollow," he said, "and we will see what it can be." They did so. They soon heard the sounds of chopping, and quickly after they heard the falling of trees. Suddenly a man came up to the place of their concealment. He stood still and gazed at them. They did the same in utter amazement. After looking at them for some time, the person advanced and extended his hand toward them. The eldest took it, and they shook hands. He then spoke, but they could not understand each other. He then cried out for his comrades. They came, and examined very minutely the dress of the travelers.

They again tried to converse. Finding it impossible, the strangers then motioned to the *Naubequon,* a small boat, wishing them to embark. They consulted with each other for a short time. The eldest then motioned that they should go on board. They embarked on board the boat, which they found to be loaded with wood. When they reached the side of the supposed island, they were surprised to see a great number of people, who all came to the side and looked at them with open mouths. One spoke out, above the others, and appeared to be the leader. He motioned them to get on board. He looked at and examined them, and took them down into the cabin, and set things before them to eat. He treated them very kindly.

When they came on deck again, all the sails were spread, and they were fast losing sight of land. In the course of the night and the following day, they were sick at the stomach, but soon recovered. When they had been out at sea ten days, they became sorrowful, as they could not converse with the strangers—those who had hats on.

The following night Iosco dreamed that his spirit appeared to him. He told him not to be discouraged, that he would open his ears, so as to be able to understand the people with hats. "I will not permit you to understand much," said he, "only sufficient to reveal your wants, and to know what is said to you." Iosco repeated this dream to his friends, and they were satisfied and encouraged by it. When they had been out about thirty days, the master of the ship motioned them to change their dresses of leather for such as his people wore; for if they did not, his master would be displeased. It was on this occasion that the elder first understood a few words of the language. The first phrase he understood was *La que notte,* and from one word to another he was soon able to speak it.

One day the men cried out, "Land!" and soon after they heard a noise resembling thunder, in repeated peals. When they had got over their fears, they were shown the large guns which made this noise. Soon after, they saw a vessel smaller than their own, sailing out of a bay, in the direction toward them. She had flags on her masts, and when she came near she fired a gun. The large vessel also hoisted her flags, and the boat came alongside. The master told the person who came in it to tell his master or king that he had six travelers on board, such as had never been seen before, and that they were coming to visit him. It was some time after the departure of this messenger before the vessel got up to the town. It was then dark, but they could see people, and horses, and vehicles ashore.

They were landed and placed in a covered vehicle, and driven off. When they stopped, they were taken into a large and splendid room. They were here told that the great chief wished to see them. They were shown into another large room, filled with men and women. All the room was of massive silver.

The chief asked them their business, and the object of their journey. They told him where they were from, and where they were going, and the nature of the enterprise which they had undertaken. He tried to dissuade them from its execution, telling them of the many trials and difficulties they would have to undergo; that so many days' march from his country dwelt a bad spirit, or Manito, who foreknew and foretold the existence and arrival of all who entered his country. It is impossible, he said, my children, for you ever to arrive at the object you are in search of.

Iosco replied, "Nosa," and they could see the chief blush in being called father, "we have come so far on our way, and we will continue it; we have resolved firmly that we will do so. We think our lives are of no value, for we have given them up for this object. Nosa," he repeated, "do not then prevent us from going on our journey." The chief then dismissed them with valuable presents, after having appointed the next day to speak to them again, and provided everything that they needed or wished for.

Next day they were again summoned to appear before the king. He again tried to dissuade them. He said he would send them back to their country in one of his vessels; but all he said had no effect. "Well," said he, "if you will go, I will furnish you all that is needed for your journey." He had everything provided accordingly. He told them that three days before they reached the bad spirit he had warned them of, they would hear his rattle. He cautioned them to be wise, for he felt that he should never see them all again.

They resumed their journey, and traveled sometimes through villages, but they soon left them behind and passed over a region of forests and plains, without inhabitants.

They found that all the productions of the new country, trees, animals, birds, were entirely different from those they were accustomed to, on the other side of the great waters. They traveled and traveled, till they wore out all of the clothing that had been given to them, and had to take to their leather clothing again.

The three days the chief spoke of meant three years, for it was only at the end of the third year that they came within the sound of the spirit's rattle. The sound appeared to be near, but they continued walking on, day after day, without apparently getting any nearer to it. Suddenly they came to a very extensive plain. They could see the blue ridges of distant mountains rising on the horizon beyond it. They pushed on, thinking to get over the plain before night, but they were overtaken by darkness. They were now on a stony part of the plain, covered by about a foot's depth of water. They were weary and fatigued. Some of them said, "Let us lie down." "No, no," said the others, "let us push on."

Soon they stood on firm ground, but it was as much as they could do to stand, for they were very weary. They, however, made an effort to encamp, lighted a fire, and refreshed themselves by eating. They then began conversing about the sound of the spirit's rattle, which they had heard for several days. Suddenly the noise began again; it sounded as if it was subterraneous, and it shook the ground. They tied up their bundles and went toward the spot. They soon came to a large building, which was illuminated. As soon as they came to the door, they were met by a rather elderly man. "How do ye do," said he, "my grandsons? Walk in, walk in; I am glad to see you; I knew when you started; I saw you encamp this evening. Sit down, and tell me the news of the country you left, for I am interested in it."

They complied with his wishes, and when they had concluded, each one presented him with a piece of tobacco. He then revealed to them things that would happen in their journey, and predicted its successful accomplishment. "I do not say that all of you," said he, "will successfully go through it. You have passed over three-fourths of your way, and I will tell you how to proceed after you get to the edge of the earth. Soon after you leave this place, you will hear a deafening sound. It is the sky descending on the edge, but it keeps moving up and down. You will watch, and when it moves up, you will see a vacant space between it and the earth. You must not be afraid. A chasm of awful depth is there, which separates the unknown from this earth, and a veil of darkness conceals it. Fear not. You must leap through; and if you succeed, you will find yourselves on a beautiful plain, and in a soft and mild light emitted by the moon." They thanked him for his advice. A pause ensued.

"I have told you the way," he said. "Now tell me again of the country you have left, for I committed dreadful ravages while I was there. Does not the country show marks of it? And do not the inhabitants tell of me to their children? I came to this place to mourn over my bad actions, and am trying, by my present course of life, to relieve my mind of the load that is on it." They told him that their fathers spoke often of a celebrated personage called Manabozho, who performed great exploits. "I am he," said the spirit. They gazed with astonishment and fear. "Do you see this pointed house?" said he, pointing to one that resembled a sugar loaf. "You can now each speak your wishes, and will be answered from that house. Speak out, and ask what each wants, and it shall be granted."

One of them, who was vain, asked with presumption that he might live forever, and never be in want. He was answered, "Your wish shall be granted." The second made the same request, and received the same answer. The third asked to live longer than common people, and to be always successful in his war excursions, never losing any of his young men. He was told, "Your wishes are granted." The fourth joined in the same request, and received the same reply. The fifth made a humble request, asking to live as long as men generally do, and that he might be crowned with such success in hunting as to be able to provide for his parents and relatives. The sixth made the same request, and it was granted to both, in pleasing tones, from the pointed house.

After hearing these responses they prepared to depart. They were told by Manabozho that they had been with him but one day, but they afterward found that they had remained there upward of a year. When they were on the point of setting out, Manabozho exclaimed, "Stop! you two, who asked me for eternal life, will receive the boon you wish immediately." He spoke, and one was turned into a stone called *Shin-gauba-wossin,* and the other into a cedar tree. "Now," said he to the others, "you can go." They left him in fear, saying, "We were fortunate to escape so, for the king told us he was wicked, and that we should not probably escape from him."

They had not proceeded far when they began to hear the sound of the beating sky. It appeared to be near at hand, but they had a long interval to travel before they came near, and the sound was then stunning to their senses; for when the sky came down, its pressure would force gusts of wind from the opening, so strong that it was with difficulty they could keep their feet, and the sun passed but a short distance above their heads. They, however, approached boldly, but had to wait some time before they could muster courage enough to leap through the dark veil that covered the passage. The sky would come down with violence, but it would rise slowly and gradually.

The two who had made the humble request stood near the edge, and with no little exertion succeeded, one after the other, in leaping through, and gaining a firm foothold. The remaining two were fearful and undecided. The others spoke to them through the darkness, saying, "Leap! leap! The sky is on its way down." These two looked up and saw it descending, but fear paralyzed their efforts; they made but a feeble attempt, so as to reach the opposite side with their hands. But the sky at the same time struck the earth with great violence and a terrible sound, and forced them into the dreadful black chasm.

The two successful adventurers, of whom Iosco now was chief, found themselves in a beautiful country, lighted by the moon, which shed around a mild and pleasant light. They could see the moon approaching as if it were from behind a hill. They advanced, and an aged woman spoke to them; she had a white face and pleasing air, and looked rather old, though she spoke to them very kindly. They knew from her first appearance that she was the Moon. She asked them several questions; she told them that she knew of their coming, and was happy to see them; she informed them that they were halfway to her brother's, and that from the earth to her abode was half the distance.

"I will, by and by, have leisure," said she, "and will go and conduct you to my brother, for he is now absent on his daily course. You will succeed in your object, and return in safety to your country and friends, with the good wishes, I am sure, of my brother." While the travelers were with her, they received every attention. When the proper time arrived, she said to them, "My brother is now rising from below, and we shall see his light as he comes over the distant edge. Come," said she, "I will lead you up." They went forward, but in some mysterious way they hardly knew how; they rose almost directly up, as if they had ascended steps. They then came upon an immense plain, declining in the direction of the Sun's approach. When he came near, the Moon spoke, "I have brought you these persons, whom we knew were coming," and with this she disappeared. The Sun motioned with his hand for them to follow him. They did so, but found it rather difficult, as the way was steep. They found it particularly so from the edge of the earth till they got halfway between that point and midday.

When they reached this spot the Sun stopped and sat down to rest. "What, my children," said he, "has brought you here? I could not speak to you before. I could not stop at any place but this, for this is my first resting place; then at the center, which is at midday, and then halfway from that to the western edge. Tell me," he continued, "the object of your undertaking this journey and all the circumstances which have happened to you on the way."

They complied. Iosco told him their main object was to see him. They had lost four of their friends on the way, and they wished to know whether they could return in safety to the earth, that they might inform their friends and relatives of all that had befallen them. They concluded by requesting him to grant their wishes. He replied, "Yes, you shall certainly return in safety; but your companions were vain and presumptuous in their demands. They were Foolish Ones. They aspired to what Manitoes only could enjoy. But you two, as I said, shall get back to your country and become as happy as the hunter's life can make you. You shall never be in want of the necessaries of life as long as you are permitted to live; and you will have the satisfaction of relating your journey to your friends, and also of telling them of me. Follow me, follow me," he said, commencing his course again.

The ascent was now gradual, and they soon came to a level plain. After traveling some time he again sat down to rest, for he had arrived at the halfway line. "You see," said he, "it is level at this place, but a short distance onward, my way descends gradually to my last resting place, from which there is an abrupt descent." He repeated his assurance that they should be shielded from danger if they relied firmly on his power. "Come here quickly," he said, placing something before them on which they could descend. "Keep firm," said he, as they resumed the descent. They went downward as if they had been let down by ropes.

In the meantime, the parents of these two young men dreamed that their sons were returning, and that they should soon see them. They placed the fullest confidence in their dreams. Early in the morning they left their lodges for a remote point in the forest, where they expected to meet them. They were not long at the place before they saw the adventurers returning, for they had descended not far from that place. The young men knew they were their fathers. The met, and were happy. They related all that had befallen them. They did not conceal anything; and they expressed their gratitude to the different Manitoes who had preserved them, by feasting and gifts, and particularly to the Sun and Moon, who had received them as their children.

Glooscap and the Three Seekers of Gifts

Of old time. Now when it was noised abroad that whoever besought Glooscap could obtain the desire of his heart, there were three men who said among themselves, "Let us seek the Master." So they left their home in the early spring when the bluebird first sang, and walked till the fall frosts, and then into winter, and ever on till the next midsummer. And having come to a small path in a great forest, they followed it, till they came out by a very beautiful river; so fair a sight they had never seen, and so went onward till it grew to be a great lake. And so they kept to the path which, when untrodden, was marked by blazed trees, the bark having been removed, in Indian fashion, on the side of the trunk which is opposite the place where the wigwam or village lies toward which it turns. So the mark can be seen as the traveler goes toward the goal, but not while leaving it.

Then after a time they came to a long point of land running out into the lake, and having ascended a high hill, they saw in the distance a smoke, which guided them to a large, well-built wigwam. And entering, they found seated on the right side a handsome, healthy man of middle age, and by the other a woman so decrepit that she seemed to be a hundred years old. Opposite the door, and on the left side, was a mat, which seemed to show that a third person had there a seat.

And the man made them welcome, and spoke as if he

were well pleased to see them, but did not ask them whence they came or whither they were going, as is wont among Indians when strangers come to their homes or are met in travel. Ere long they heard the sound of a paddle, and then the noise of a canoe being drawn ashore. And there came in a youth of fine form and features and well clad, bearing weapons as if from hunting, who addressed the old woman as *Kejoo*—or mother—and told her that he had brought game. And with sore ado—for she was feeble—the old dame tottered out and brought in four beavers; but she was so much troubled to cut them up that the elder, saying to the younger man, "*Uoh-keen!*—My brother," bade him do the work. And they supped on beaver.

So they remained for a week, resting themselves, for they were sadly worn with their wearisome journey, and also utterly ragged. And then a wondrous thing came to pass, which first taught them that they were in an enchanted land. For one morning the elder man bade the younger wash their mother's face. And as he did this all her wrinkles vanished, and she became young and very beautiful; in all their lives the travelers had never seen so lovely a woman. Her hair, which had been white and scanty, now hung to her feet, dark and glossy as a blackbird's breast. Then, having been clad in fine array, she showed a tall, lithe, and graceful form at its best.

And the travelers said to themselves, "Truly this man is a great magician!" They all walked forth to see the place. Never was sunshine so pleasantly tempered by a soft breeze; for all in that land was fair, and it grew fairer day by day to all who dwelt there. Tall trees with rich foliage and fragrant flowers, but without lower limbs or underbrush, grew as in a grove, wide as a forest, yet so far apart that the eye could pierce the distance in every direction.

Now when they felt for the first time that they were in a new life and a magic land, he that was host asked them whence they came and what they sought. So they said that they sought Glooscap. And the host replied, "Lo, I am he!" And they were awed by his presence, for a great glory and majesty now sat upon him. As the woman had changed, so had he, for all in that place was wonderful.

Then the first, telling what he wanted, said, "I am a wicked man, and I have a bad temper. I am prone to wrath and reviling, yet I would fain be pious, meek, and holy."

And the next said, "I am very poor, and my life is hard. I toil, but can barely make my living. I would fain be rich."

Now the third replied, "I am of low estate, being despised and hated by all my people, and I wish to be loved and respected." And to all these the Master made answer, "So shall it be!"

And taking his medicine bag he gave unto each a small box, and bade them keep it closed until they should be once more at home. And on returning to the wigwam he also gave to each of them new garments; in all their lives they had never seen or heard of such rich apparel or such ornaments as they now had. Then when it was time to depart, as they knew not the way to their home, he arose and went with them. Now they had been more than a year in coming. But he, having put on his belt, went forth, and they followed, till in the forenoon he led them to the top of a high mountain, from which in the distance they beheld yet another, the blue outline of which could just be seen above the horizon. And having been told that their way was unto it, they thought it would be a week's journey to reach it. But they went on, and in the middle of the afternoon of the same day they were there, on the summit of the second mountain. And looking from this afar, all was familiar to them—hill and river, and wood and lakes—all was in their memory. "And there," said the Master, pointing unto it, "there is your village!" So he left them alone, and they went on their way, and before the sun had set were safe at home.

Yet when they came, no one knew them, because of the great change in their appearance and their fine attire, the like of which had never been seen by man in those days. But having made themselves known to their friends, all that were there of old and young gathered together to gaze upon and hear what they had to say. And they were amazed.

Then each of them, having opened his box, found therein an unguent, rich and fragrant, and with this they rubbed their bodies completely. And they were ever after so fragrant from the divine anointing that all sought to be near them. Happy were they who could but sniff at the blessed smell which came from them.

Now he who had been despised for his deformity and weakness and meanness became beautiful and strong and stately as a pine tree. There was no man in all the land so graceful or of such good behavior.

And he who had desired abundance had it, in all fullness, his wish. For the moose and caribou came to him in the forest, the fish leaped into his nets; all men gave unto him, and he gave unto all freely, to the end.

And he that had been wicked and of evil mind, hasty and cruel, became meek and patient, good and gentle, and he made others like himself. And he had his reward, for there was a blessing upon him as upon all those who had wished wisely even unto the end of their days.

The Boy Who Saw A-ti-us

Many years ago the Pawnees started on their winter hunt. The buffalo were scarce, and the people could get hardly any meat. It was very cold, and the snow lay deep on the ground. The tribe traveled southward, and crossed the Republican, but still found no buffalo. They had eaten all the dried meat and all the corn that they had brought with them, and now they were starving. The sufferings of the people were great, and the little ones began to die of hunger. Now they began to eat their robes, and parfleches, and moccasins.

There was in the tribe a boy about sixteen years old, who was all alone and was very poor. He had no relations who could take care of him, and he lived with a woman whose husband had been killed by the Sioux. She had two children, a boy and a girl; and she had a good heart, and was sorry for the poor boy. In this time of famine, these people had scarcely anything to eat, and whenever the boy got hold of any food, he gave it to the woman, who divided it among them all.

The tribe kept traveling southward looking for buffalo, but they had to go very slowly, because they were all so weak. Still they found no buffalo, and each day the young men that were sent out to look for them climbed the highest hills, and came back at night, and reported that they could only see the white prairie covered with snow. All this time little ones were dying of hunger, and the men and women were growing weaker every day.

The poor boy suffered with the rest, and at last he became so weak that he hardly could keep up with the camp, even though it moved very slowly. One morning he was hardly able to help the old woman pack the lodge, and after it had been packed, he went back to the fire, and sat down beside it, and watched the camp move slowly off across the valley, and up over the bluffs. He thought to himself, "Why should I go on? I can't keep up for more than a day or two longer anyhow. I may as well stay here and die." So he gathered together the ends of the sticks that lay by the fire, and put them on the coals, and spread his hands over the blaze, and rubbed them together and got warm, and then lay down by the fire. Pretty soon he went to sleep.

When he came to himself, it was about the middle of the day, and as he looked toward the sky he saw two spots there between him and the sun, and he wondered what they were. As he looked at them, they became larger and larger, and at last he could see that they were birds; and by and by, as they came still nearer, he saw that they were two swans. The swans kept coming lower and lower, and at last they alighted on the ground right by the fire, and walked up to where the boy lay. He was so weak he could not get up, and they came to him, one on each side, and stooped down, and pushed their shoulders under him, and raised him up and put him on their backs, and then spread their broad wings, and flew away upward. Then the boy went to sleep again.

When he awoke he was lying on the ground before a very big lodge. It was large and high, and on it were painted pictures of many strange animals, in beautiful colors. The boy had never seen such a fine lodge. The air was warm here, and he felt stronger than before. He tried to raise himself up, and after trying once or twice he got on his feet, and walked to the door of the lodge, and went in. Opposite the door sat A-ti-us. He was very large and very handsome, and his face was kind and gentle. He was dressed in beautiful clothes, and wore a white buffalo robe. Behind him, from the lodge poles, hung many strange weapons. Around the lodge on one side sat many chiefs, and doctors, and warriors. They all wore fine clothes of white buckskin, embroidered with beautifully colored quills. Their robes were all of beaver skin, very beautiful.

When the boy entered the lodge, A-ti-us said to him, "*Looah, pi-rau, we-tus suks-pit*—Welcome, my son, and sit down." And he said to one of the warriors, "Give him something to eat." The warrior took down a beautifully painted sack of parfleche, and took his knife from its sheath, and cut off a piece of dried meat about as big as one's two fingers, and a piece of fat about the same size, and gave them to the boy. The boy, who was so hungry, thought that this was not very much to give to one who was starving, but took it, and began to eat. He put the fat on the lean, and cut the pieces off, and ate for a long time. But after he had eaten for a long time, the pieces of meat remained the same size; and he ate all that he wanted, and then put the pieces down, still the same size.

After the boy had finished eating, A-ti-us spoke to him. He told him that he had seen the sufferings of his people, and had been sorry for them; and then he told the boy what to do. So he kept the boy there for a little while longer, and gave him some fine new clothing and weapons. And then he told one of the warriors to send the boy back; and the warrior led him out of the lodge to where the swans were standing near the entrance, and the boy got onto their backs. Then the warrior put his hand on his face, and pressed his eyelids together, and the boy went to sleep. And by and by the boy awoke, and found himself alone by the fire. The fire had gone out, but the ground was still covered with snow, and it was very cold.

Now the boy felt strong, and he stood up, and started running along the trail which the camp had taken. That night after dark he overtook the camp, for they traveled very slowly, and he walked through the village till he came to the lodge where the woman was, and went in. She was surprised to see him in his new clothes, and looking so well and strong, and told him to sit down. There was a little fire in the lodge, and the boy could see that the woman was cutting up something into small pieces with her knife.

The boy said to her, "What are you doing?"

She answered, "I am going to boil our last piece of robe. After we have eaten this, there will be nothing left, and we can then only die."

The boy said nothing, but watched her for a little while, and then stood up and went out of the lodge. The door had hardly fallen behind him, when the woman heard a buffalo coughing, and then the breaking of the crisp snow, as if a heavy weight was settling on it. In a moment the boy lifted the lodge door, and came in, and sat down by the fire, and said to the woman, "Go out and bring in some meat." The woman looked at him, for she was astonished, but he said nothing; so she went out, and there in the snow by the side of the lodge was a fat buffalo cow. Tnen the woman's heart was glad. She skinned the cow, and brought some of the meat into the lodge and cooked it, and they all ate and were satisfied. The woman was good, so she sent her son to the lodges of all her relations, and all her friends, and told them all to come next morning to her lodge to a feast, "for," she said, "I have plenty of meat."

So the next morning all her relations and all her friends came, so many that they could not all get into the lodge; some had to stand outside, but they ate with her. She cooked the meat of the cow for them, and they ate until it was all gone, and they were satisfied. And after they had done eating, they lighted their pipes and prayed, saying, "*A-ti-us, we-tus kit-tah-we*—Father, you are the ruler."

While they were smoking, the poor boy called the woman's son to him, and pointed to a high hill near the camp, and said, "*Looah, suks-kus-sis-pah ti-rah hah-tur*— Run hard to the top of that hill, and tell me what you see." So the boy threw off his robe, and smoothed back his hair, and started, and ran as hard as he could over the snow to the top of the hill. When he got there, he shaded his eyes with his hand, for the sun shone bright on the snow and blinded him, and he looked east, and west, and north, and south, but he could see nothing but the shining white snow on the prairie. After he had looked all ways, he ran back as hard as he could to the village. When he came to the lodge, he went to the poor boy, and said to him, "I don't see anything but the snow." The poor boy said, "You don't look good. Go again." So the boy started again, and ran as hard as he could to the hilltop, and when he got there, panting, he looked all ways, long and carefully, but still he could see nothing but the snow. So he turned and ran back to the village, and told the poor boy again that he saw nothing. The boy said, "You don't look good."

Then he took his bow in his hand, and put his quiver on his back, and drew his robe up under his arm so that he could run well, and started himself, and ran as hard as he could to the top of the hill. When he got there he looked off to the south, and there, as far as he could see, the plain was black with buffalo struggling in the deep snow. And he turned to the village, and signaled them with his robe that buffalo were in sight. In a few minutes all the Pawnees had seized their bows and arrows, and were running toward him, and the women fixed the travois, and took their knives, and followed.

The boy waited on the hilltop until the warriors came up, and then they went down to the buffalo, running on the snow. The buffalo could not get away on account of the deep snow, and the Pawnees made a great killing. Plenty of fat meat they got, enough to last them until the summer hunt, and plenty of warm winter robes. They did not have to move any farther, but stayed right there, killing meat and drying it until they were all fat and strong again.

And the poor boy became a great doctor in the tribe, and got rich.

Before this the Pawnees had always had a woman chief, but when the woman who was chief died, she named the poor boy as her successor, and the people made him head chief of the tribe.

The Star Family,
or
The Celestial Sisters

Waupee, the White Hawk, lived in a remote part of the forest, where animals and birds were abundant. Every day he returned from the chase with the reward of his toil, for he was one of the most skillful and celebrated hunters of his tribe. With a tall, manly form, and the fire of youth beaming from his eye, there was no forest too gloomy for him to penetrate, and no track made by the numerous kinds of birds and beasts which he could not follow.

One day he penetrated beyond any point which he had before visited. He traveled through an open forest, which enabled him to see a great distance. At length he beheld a light breaking through the foliage, which made him sure that he was on the borders of a prairie. It was a wide plain covered with grass and flowers. After walking some time without a path, he suddenly came to a ring worn through the sod, as if it had been made by footsteps following a circle. But what excited his surprise was that there was no path leading to or from it. Not the least trace of footsteps could be found, even in a crushed leaf or broken twig.

He thought he would hide himself, and lie in wait to see what this circle meant. Presently he heard the faint sounds of music in the air. He looked up in the direction they came from, and saw a small object descending from above. At first it looked like a mere speck, but rapidly increased, and

74

as it came down, the music became plainer and sweeter. It assumed the form of a basket, and was filled with twelve sisters of the most lovely forms and enchanting beauty. As soon as the basket touched the ground, they leaped out, and began to dance round the magic ring, striking, as they did so, a shining ball as we strike the drum.

Waupee gazed upon their graceful forms and motions from his place of concealment. He admired them all, but was most pleased with the youngest. Unable longer to restrain his admiration, he rushed out and endeavored to seize her. But the sisters, with the quickness of birds, the moment they descried the form of a man, leaped back into the basket and were drawn up into the sky.

Regretting his ill luck and indiscretion, he gazed till he saw them disappear, and then said, "They are gone, and I shall see them no more." He returned to his solitary lodge, but found no relief to his mind. Next day he went back to the prairie, and took his station near the ring; but in order to deceive the sisters, he assumed the form of an opossum.

He had not waited long, when he saw the wicker car descend, and heard the same sweet music. They commenced the same sportive dance, and seemed even more beautiful and graceful than before. He crept slowly toward the ring, but the instant the sisters saw him they were startled, and sprang into their car. It rose but a short distance, when one of the elder sister spoke. "Perhaps," said she, "it is come to show us how the game is played by mortals." "Oh, no!" the youngest replied. "Quick, let us ascend." And all joining in a chant, they rose out of sight.

Waupee returned to his own form again, and walked sorrowfully back to his lodge. But the night seemed a very long one, and he went back betimes the next day. He reflected upon the sort of plan to follow to secure success. He found an old stump near by, in which there were a number of mice. He thought their small form would not create alarm, and accordingly assumed it. He brought the stump and set it up near the ring. The sisters came down and resumed their sport. "But see," cried the youngest sister, "that stump was not there before." She ran affrighted toward the car. They only smiled, and gathering round the stump, struck it in jest, when out ran the mice, and Waupee among the rest. They killed them all but one, which was pursued by the youngest sister; but just as she had raised her stick to kill it, the form of Waupee arose, and he clasped his prize in his arms. The other eleven sprang to their basket and were drawn up to the skies.

He exerted all his skill to please his bride and win her affections. He wiped the tears from her eyes. He related his adventures in the chase. He dwelt upon the charms of life on the earth. He was incessant in his attentions, and picked out the way for her to walk as he led her gently toward his lodge. He felt his heart glow with joy as she entered it, and from that moment he was one of the happiest of men.

Winter and summer passed rapidly away, and their happiness was increased by the addition of a beautiful boy to their lodge. She was a daughter of one of the stars, and as the scenes of earth began to pall, she sighed to revisit her father. But she was obliged to hide these feelings from her husband. She remembered the charm that would carry her up, and took occasion, while Waupee was engaged in the chase, to construct a wicker basket, which she kept concealed. In the meantime, she collected such rarities from the earth as she thought would please her father, as well as the most dainty kinds of food. When all was in readiness, she went out one day, while Waupee was absent, to the charmed ring, taking her little son with her. As soon as they got into the car, she commenced her song and the basket rose.

As the song was wafted by the wind, it caught her husband's ear. It was a voice which he well knew, and he instantly ran to the prairie. But he could not reach the ring before he saw his wife and child ascend. He lifted up his voice in loud appeals, but they were unavailing. The basket still went up. He watched it till it became a small speck, and finally it vanished in the sky. He then bent his head down to the ground, and was miserable.

Waupee bewailed his loss through a long winter and a long summer. But he found no relief. He mourned his wife's loss sorely, but his son's still more. In the meantime, his wife had reached her home in the stars, and almost forgot, in the blissful employments there, that she had left a husband on the earth. She was reminded of this by the presence of her son, who, as he grew up, became anxious to visit the scene of his birth.

His grandfather said to his daughter one day, "Go, my child, and take your son down to his father, and ask him to come up and live with us. But tell him to bring along a specimen of each kind of bird and animal he kills in the chase." She accordingly took the boy and descended. Waupee, who was ever near the enchanted spot, heard her voice as she came down the sky. His heart beat with impatience as he saw her form and that of his son, and they were soon clasped in his arms.

He heard the message of the Star Chief, and began to hunt with the greatest activity, that he might collect the present. He spent whole nights, as well as days, in searching for every curious and beautiful bird or animal. He only preserved a tail, foot, or wing of each, to identify the species; and, when all was ready, they went to the circle and were carried up.

Great joy was manifested on their arrival at the starry plains. The Star Chief invited all his people to a feast, and, when they had assembled, he proclaimed aloud that each one might take of the earthly gifts such as he liked best. A very strange confusion immediately arose. Some chose a foot, some a wing, some a tail, and some a claw. Those who selected tails or claws were changed into animals, and ran off; the others assumed the form of birds, and flew away.

Waupee chose a white hawk's feather. His wife and son followed his example, and each one became a white hawk. Pleased with his transformation and new vitality, the chief spread out gracefully his white wings, and followed by his wife and son, descended to the earth, where the species are still to be found.

The Moqui Boy and the Eagle

The Eagle is Kah-bay-deh, commander of all that flies, and his feathers are strongest in medicine.

So long ago that no man can tell how long, there lived in Moqui an old man and an old woman, who had two children, a boy and a girl. The boy, whose name was Tai-oh, had a pet Eagle, of which he was very fond; and the Eagle loved its young master. Despite his youth, Tai-oh was an excellent hunter, and every day he brought home not only rabbits enough for the family but also to keep the Eagle well fed.

One day when he was about to start on a hunt, he asked his sister to look out for the Eagle during his absence. No sooner was he out of sight than the girl began to upbraid the bird bitterly, saying, "How I hate you, for my brother loves you so much. If it were not for you, he would give me many more rabbits, but now you eat them up."

The Eagle, feeling the injustice of this, was angry; so when she brought him a rabbit for breakfast the Eagle turned his head and looked at it sidewise, and would not touch it. At noon, when she brought him his dinner, he did the same thing; and at night, when Tai-oh returned, the Eagle told him all that had happened.

"Now," said the Eagle, "I am very tired of staying always here in Moqui, and I want to go home to visit my people a little. Come and go along with me, that you may see where the Eagle people live."

"It is well," replied Tai-oh. "Tomorrow morning we will go together."

In the morning they all went out into the fields, far down in the valley, to hoe their corn, leaving Tai-oh at home.

"Now," said the Eagle, "untie this throng from my leg, friend, and get astride my neck, and we will go."

The string was soon untied, and Tai-oh got astride the neck of the great bird, which rose up into the air as though it carried no weight at all. It circled over the town a long time, and the people cried out with wonder and fear at seeing an Eagle with a boy on his back. Then they sailed out over the fields where Tai-oh's parents and his sister were at work; and all three began to cry, and went home in great sorrow.

The Eagle kept soaring up and up until they came to the very sky. There in the blue was a little door, through which the Eagle flew. Alighting on the floor of the sky, he let Tai-oh down from his back, and said, "Now, you wait here, friend, while I go and see my people," and off he flew.

Tai-oh waited three days, and still the Eagle did not return; so he became uneasy and started out to see what he could find. After wandering a long way, he met an old Spider woman.

"Where are you going, my son?" she asked.

"I am trying to find my friend, the Eagle."

"Very well, then, I will help you. Come into my house."

"But how can I come into so small a door?" objected Tai-oh.

"Just put your foot in, and it will open big enough for you to enter."

So Tai-oh put his foot in, and, sure enough, the door opened wide, and he went into the Spider's house and sat down.

"Now," said she, "you will have some trouble in getting to the house of your friend, the Eagle, for to get there you will have to climb a dreadful ladder. It is well that you came to me for help, for that ladder is set with sharp arrowheads and knives of flint, so that if you tried to go up it, it would cut your legs off. But I will give you this sack of sacred herbs to help you. When you come to the ladder, you must chew some of the herbs and spit the juice on the ladder, which will at once become smooth for you."

Tai-oh thanked the Spider woman and started off with the sack. After a while he came to the foot of a great ladder, which went away up out of sight. Its sides and rungs were bristling with keen arrowheads, so that no living thing could climb it; but when Tai-oh chewed some of the magic herb and spat upon the ladder, all the sharp points fell off, and it was so smooth that he climbed it without a single scratch.

After a long, long climb, he came to the top of the ladder, and stepped upon the roof of the Eagle's house. But when he came to the door he found it so bristling with arrow points that whoever might try to enter would be cut to pieces. Again he chewed some of the herb, and spat upon the door; and at once all the points fell off, and he entered safely, and inside he found his Eagle friend and all the Eagle people. His friend had fallen in love with an Eagle girl and married her, and that was the reason he had not returned sooner.

Tai-oh stayed there some time, being very nicely entertained, and enjoyed himself greatly in the strange sky country. At last one of the wise old Eagle men came to him and said, "Now, my son, it is well that you go home, for your parents are very sad, thinking you are dead. After this, whenever you see an Eagle caught and kept captive, you must let it go; for now you have been in our country, and know that when we come home we take off our feather coats and are people like your own."

So Tai-oh went to his Eagle friend and said he thought he must go home.

"Very well," said the Eagle; "get on my back and shut your eyes, and we will go."

So he got on, and they went down out of the sky, and down and down until at last they came to Moqui. There the Eagle let Tai-oh down among the wondering people, and bidding him an affectionate good-by, flew off to his young wife in the sky.

Tai-oh went to his home loaded down with dried meat and tanned buckskin, which the Eagle had given him; and there was great rejoicing, for all had given him up as dead. And this is why, to this very day, the Moquis will not keep an eagle captive, though nearly all the other Pueblo towns have all the eagle prisoners they can get.

The Hermit Thrush

Long ago the birds had no songs. Only man could sing, and every morning man would greet the rising sun with a song. The birds, as they were flying by, would often stop and listen to the beautiful songs of man. In their hearts they wished that they too could sing. One day the Good Spirit visited the earth, inspecting the various things that he had created. As he walked through the forest, he noticed that there was a strange silence. Something seemed to be missing.

As the Good Spirit pondered, the sun sank behind the western hills. From the direction of the river, where there was an Indian village, there sounded the deep, rich tones of an Indian drum followed by the sacred chanting of the sunset song. The Good Spirit listened. The song was pleasing to the ears of the Good Spirit. As he looked around, he noticed that the birds were also listening to the singing. "That is what is missing," said the Good Spirit. "Birds should also have songs."

The next day the Good Spirit called all the birds to a great council. From near and far they came. The sky was filled with flying birds. The trees and bushes bent to the earth under the weight of so many.

On the great Council Rock sat the Good Spirit. He waited until all of the birds had perched and had become quiet. The Good Spirit spoke. He asked the birds if they would like to have songs, songs such as the Indian people sang. With one accord the birds all chirped, "Yes, yes!"

"Very well," said the Good Spirit. "Tomorrow when the sun rises in the east, you are all to fly up in the sky. You are to fly as high as you can. When you can fly no higher you will find your song. That bird who flies the highest will have the most beautiful song of all the birds." Saying these words, the Good Spirit vanished.

Next morning, long before sunrise, the birds were ready. There were birds everywhere. The earth was covered with them. There was great excitement. However, one little bird was very unhappy. He was the little brown thrush. Perched beside him was the great eagle. As the little bird gazed at the eagle he thought, "What chance have I to compete with this great bird? I am so little and eagle is so large. I will never be able to fly as high as he."

As he was thus thinking, an idea entered his mind, "Eagle is so excited that he will not notice me." With this thought in mind, the little brown bird flew like a flash to the eagle's head and quickly hid under his feathers. The great eagle was so excited that he did not notice the little thrush. "With my great wings, I will surely win," thought he.

The sun finally looked over the eastern hill. With a great roar of wings the many birds took off. The air was so full of flying birds that for a time the sky was dark. Their bodies covered the face of the sun.

For a long time the birds flew upward. Finally the smaller, weaker, birds began to tire. The little hummingbird was the first to give up. His little wings beat the air so hard that to this day one can, if one listens, hear his humming wings. His little squeaking calls say, "Wait, wait for me," a very plain song.

The fat cowbird was the next to give up. As he floated down, he listened and heard his song, a very common song. Other birds weakened and while flying earthward, listened and learned their songs.

At last the sun was at the end of the earth. The night sky began to darken the earth. By this time there were only a few birds left. They were the large, stronger-winged birds, the eagle, hawk, owl, buzzard, and loon. All night the birds flew up, ever up. When the sun rose next morning only the eagle, chief of all birds, was left. He was still going strong.

When the sun was halfway in the sky, he began to tire. Finally, with a look of triumph, for there were no other birds in sight, the tired eagle began to soar earthward. The little thrush, riding under the feathers of the great eagle, had been asleep all of this time. When the eagle started back to earth the little thrush awoke. He hopped off the eagle's head and began to fly upward. Eagle saw him go and glared with anger at him, but was powerless to stop him as he was completely exhausted.

The little thrush flew up and up. He soon came to a hole in the sky. He found himself in a beautiful country, the Happy Hunting Grounds. As he entered the Spirit World he heard a beautiful song. He stayed in heaven for a while learning this song. When he had learned it completely, he left the Land of Happy Spirits and flew back toward earth. He could hardly wait to reach the earth. He was anxious to show off his beautiful song.

As the thrush neared the earth he glanced down at the Council Rock. There sat all of the birds, and on the Council Rock, glaring up at him was Akweks, the eagle. All the birds were very silent as they waited for thrush to light on the council ground. Suddenly the feeling of glory left the little thrush and he felt ashamed. He knew that he had cheated to get his beautiful song. He also feared Akweks, who might get even with him for stealing a free ride. He flew in silence to the deep woods, and in shame, with dragging heart, hid under the branches of the largest tree. He was so ashamed that he wanted no one to see him.

There you will find him today. Never does the hermit thrush come out into the open. He is still ashamed because he cheated. Sometimes, however, he cannot restrain himself, and he must sing his beautiful song. When he does this the other birds cease their singing. Well they know that the song of the hermit thrush, the song from heaven, will make their songs sound very weak.

That is why the hermit thrush is so shy. That is why his song is the most beautiful song of all the birds. That is why this spirit song causes the sun to shine in the hearts of the Indian people who hear it as they go into the dark forest.

The Rabbit Huntress
and Her Adventures

It was long ago, in the days of the ancients, that a poor maiden lived at Kyawana Tehua-tsana—Little Gateway of Zuñi River. You know there are black stone walls of houses standing there on the tops of the cliffs of lava, above the narrow place through which the river runs, to this day.

In one of these houses there lived this poor maiden alone with her feeble old father and her aged mother. She was unmarried, and her brothers had all been killed in wars, or had died gently. So the family lived there helplessly, so far as many things were concerned, from the lack of men in their house.

It is true that in making the gardens—the little plantings of beans, pumpkins, squashes, melons, and corn—the maiden was able to do very well; and thus mainly on the products of these things the family were supported. But, as in those days of our ancients we had neither sheep nor cattle, the hunt was depended upon to supply the meat; or sometimes it was procured by barter of the products of the fields to those who hunted mostly. Of these things, this little family had barely enough for their own subsistence; hence, they could not procure their supplies of meat in this way.

Long before, it had been a great house, for many were the brave and strong young men who had lived in it; but the rooms were now empty, or at best contained only the leavings of those who had lived there, much used and worn out.

One autumn day, near wintertime, snow fell, and it became very cold. The maiden had gathered brush and firewood in abundance, and it was piled along the roof of the house and down underneath the ladder which descended from the top. She saw the young men issue forth the next morning in great numbers, their feet protected by long stockings of deerskin, the fur turned inward, and they carried on their shoulders and stuck in their belts stone axes and rabbit sticks.

As she gazed at them from the roof, she said to herself, "O that I were a man and could go forth, as do these young men, hunting rabbits! Then my poor old mother and father would not lack for flesh with which to duly season their food and nourish their lean bodies." Thus ran her thoughts, and before night, as she saw these same young men coming in, one after another, some of them bringing long strings of rabbits, others short ones, but none of them empty-handed, she decided that, woman though she was, she would set forth on the morrow to try what luck she might find in the killing of rabbits herself.

It may seem strange that, although this maiden was beautiful and young, the youths did not give her some of their rabbits. But their feelings were not friendly, for no one of them would she accept as a husband, although one after another of them had offered himself for marriage.

Fully resolved, the girl that evening sat down by the fireplace, and turning toward her aged parents, said, "O my mother and father, I see that the snow has fallen, whereby easily rabbits are tracked, and the young men who went out this morning returned long before evening heavily laden with strings of this game. Behold, in the other rooms of our house are many rabbit sticks, and there hang on the walls stone axes, and with these I might perchance strike down a rabbit on his trail, or, if he run into a log, split the log and dig him out. So I have thought during the day, and have decided to go tomorrow and try my fortunes in the hunt, woman though I be."

"Naiya, my daughter," quavered the feeble old mother,

"you would surely be very cold, or you would lose your way, or grow so tired that you could not return before night, and you must not go out to hunt rabbits, woman as you are."

"Why, certainly not," insisted the old man, rubbing his lean knees and shaking his head over the days that were gone. "No, no; let us live in poverty rather than that you should run such risks as these, O my daughter."

But say what they would, the girl was determined. And the old man said at last, "Very well! You will not be turned from your course. Therefore, O daughter, I will help you as best I may." He hobbled into another room, and found there some old deerskins covered thickly with fur; and drawing them out, he moistened and carefully softened them, and cut out for the maiden long stockings, which he sewed up with sinew and the fiber of the yucca leaf. Then he selected for her from among the old possessions of his brothers and sons, who had been killed or perished otherwise, a number of rabbit sticks and a fine, heavy stone axe. Meanwhile, the old woman busied herself in preparing a lunch for the girl, which was composed of little cakes of corn meal, spiced with pepper and wild onions, pierced through the middle, and baked in the ashes. When she had made a long string of these by threading them like beads on a rope of yucca fiber, she laid them down not far from the ladder on a little bench, with the rabbit sticks, the stone axe, and the deerskin stockings.

That night the maiden planned and planned, and early on the following morning, even before the young men had gone out from the town, she had put on a warm, short-skirted dress, knotted a mantle over her shoulder and thrown another and larger one over her back, drawn on the deerskin stockings, had thrown the string of corn-cakes over her shoulder, stuck the rabbit sticks in her belt, and carrying the stone axe in her hand sallied forth eastward through the Gateway of Zuñi and into the plain of the valley beyond, called the Plain of the Burnt River, on account of the black, roasted-looking rocks along some parts of its sides. Dazzlingly white the snow stretched out before her—not deep, but unbroken—and when she came near the cliffs with many little canyons in them, along the northern side of the valley, she saw many a trail of rabbits running out and in among the rocks and between the bushes.

Warm and excited by her unwonted exercise, she did not heed a coming snowstorm, but ran about from one place to another, following the trails of the rabbits, sometimes up into the canyons, where the forests of piñon and cedar stood, and where here and there she had the good fortune sometimes to run two, three, or four rabbits into a single hollow log. It was little work to split these logs, for they were small, as you know, and to dig out the rabbits and slay them by a blow of the hand on the nape of the neck, back of the ears. As she killed each rabbit she raised it reverently to her lips, and breathed from its nostrils its expiring breath, and tying its legs together, placed it on the string, which after a while began to grow heavy on her shoulders.

Still she kept on, little heeding the snow which was falling fast; nor did she notice that it was growing darker and darker, so intent was she on the hunt, and so glad was she to capture so many rabbits. Indeed, she followed the trails until they were no longer visible, as the snow fell all around her, thinking all the while, "How happy will be my poor old father and mother that they shall now have flesh to eat! How strong will they grow! And when this meat is gone, that which is dried and preserved of it also, lo! another snowstorm will no doubt come, and I can go hunting again."

At last the twilight came, and looking around, she found that the snow had fallen deeply, there was no trail, and that she had lost her way. True, she turned about and started in the direction of her home, as she supposed, walking as fast as she could through the soft, deep snow. Yet she reckoned not rightly, for instead of going eastward along the valley, she went southward across it; and entering the mouth of the Descending Plain of the Pines, she went on and on, thinking she was going homeward, until at last it grew dark and she knew not which way to turn.

"What harm," thought she, "if I find a sheltered place among the rocks? What harm if I remain all night, and go home in the morning when the snow has ceased falling, and by the light I shall know my way?"

So she turned about to some rocks which appeared, black and dim, a short distance away. Fortunately, among these rocks is the cave which is known as Taiuma's Cave. This she came to, and peering into that black hole, she saw in it, back some distance, a little glowing light. "Ha, ha!" thought she, "perhaps some rabbit hunters like myself, belated yesterday, passed the night here and left the fire burning. If so, this is greater good fortune than I could have looked for." So, lowering the string of rabbits which she carried on her shoulder, and throwing off her mantle, she crawled in, peering well into the darkness, for fear of wild beasts; then, returning, she drew in the string of rabbits and the mantle.

Indeed, there was a bed of hot coals buried in the ashes in the very middle of the cave, and piled up on one side were fragments of broken wood. The girl, happy in her good fortune, issued forth and gathered more sticks from the cliff side, where dead piñons are found in great numbers, and bringing them in little armfuls one after another, she finally succeeded in gathering a store sufficient to keep the fire burning brightly all the night through. Then she drew off her snow-covered stockings of deerskin and the bedraggled mantles, and building a fire, hung them up to dry and sat down to rest herself. The fire burned up and glowed brightly, so that the whole cave was as light as a room at night when a dance is being celebrated. By and by, after her clothing had dried, she spread a mantle on the floor of the cave by the side of the fire, and sitting down, dressed one of her rabbits and roasted it, and, untying the string of corncakes her mother had made for her, feasted on the roasted meat and cakes.

She had just finished her evening meal, and was about to recline and watch the fire for a while, when she heard away off in the distance a long, low cry of distress—*"Ho-o-o-o thlaia-a!"*

"Ah," thought the girl, "someone, more belated than myself, is lost; doubtless one of the rabbit hunters." She got up, and went nearer to the entrance of the cavern.

"Ho-o-o-o thlaia-a!" sounded the cry, nearer this time. She ran out, and as it was repeated again, she placed her hand to her mouth, and cried, woman though she was, as loudly as possible, *"Li-i thlaia-a! Here!"*

The cry was repeated near at hand, and presently the maiden, listening first, and then shouting, and listening again, heard the clatter of an enormous rattle. In dismay and terror she threw her hands into the air, and, crouching down, rushed into the cave and retreated to its farthest limits, where she sat shuddering with fear. For she knew that one of the Cannibal Demons of those days, perhaps the renowned Atahsaia of the east, had seen the light of her fire through the cave entrance, with his terrible staring eyes, and assuming it to be a lost wanderer, had cried out, and so led her to guide him to her place of concealment.

On came the Demon, snapping the twigs under his feet and shouting in a hoarse, loud voice, *"Ho lithlsh ta ime!—* Ho, there! So you are in here, are you?" *Kothl!* clanged his rattle, while almost fainting with terror, closer to the rock crouched the maiden.

The old Demon came to the entrance of the cave and bawled out, "I am cold, I am hungry! Let me in!" Without further ado, he stooped and tried to get in; but behold! the entrance was too small for his giant shoulders to pass. Then he pretended to be wonderfully civil, and said, "Come out, and bring me something to eat."

"I have nothing for you," cried the maiden. "I have eaten my food."

"Have you no rabbits?"

"Yes."

"Come out and bring me some of them."

But the maiden was so terrified that she dared not move toward the entrance.

"Throw me a rabbit!" shouted the old Demon.

The maiden threw him one of her precious rabbits at last, when she could rise and go to it. He clutched it with his long, horny hand, gave one gulp and swallowed it. Then he cried out, "Throw me another!" She threw him another, which he also immediately swallowed; and so on until the poor maiden had thrown all the rabbits to the voracious old monster. Every one she threw him he caught in his huge, yellow-tusked mouth, and swallowed, hair and all, at one gulp.

"Throw me another!" cried he, when the last had already been thrown to him.

So the poor maiden was forced to say, "I have no more."

"Throw me your overshoes!" cried he.

She threw the overshoes of deerskin, and these like the rabbits he speedily devoured. Then he called for her moccasins, and she threw them; for her belt, and she threw it; and finally, wonderful to tell, she threw even her mantle, and blanket, and her overdress, until, behold, she had nothing left!

Now, with all that he had eaten, the old Demon was swollen hugely at the stomach, and though he tried and tried to squeeze himself through the mouth of the cave, he could not by any means succeed. Finally, lifting his great flint axe, he began to shatter the rock about the entrance to the cave, and slowly but surely he enlarged the hole and the maiden now knew that as soon as he could get in he would devour her also, and she almost fainted at the sickening thought. Pound, pound, pound, pound, went the great axe of the Demon as he struck the rocks.

In the distance the two War-gods were sitting in their home at Thla-uthla—the Shrine amid the Bushes— beyond Thunder Mountain, and though far off, they heard thus in the middle of the night the pounding of the Demon's hammer axe against the rocks. And of course they knew at once that a poor maiden, for the sake of her father and mother, had been out hunting; that she had lost her way, and finding a cave where there was a little fire, entered it, rebuilt the fire, and rested herself; that attracted by the light of her fire, the Cannibal Demon had come and besieged her retreat, and only a little time hence would he so enlarge the entrance to the cave that he could squeeze even his great over-filled paunch through it and come at the maiden to destroy her. So, catching up their wonderful weapons, these two War-gods flew away into the darkness and in no time they were approaching the Descending Plain of the Pines.

Just as the Demon was about to enter the cavern, and the maiden had fainted at seeing his huge face and gray shock of hair and staring eyes, his yellow, protruding tusks, and his horny, taloned hand, they came upon the old beast; and each one hitting him a welt with his war club, they "ended his daylight," and then hauled him forth into the open space. They opened his huge paunch and withdrew from it the maiden's garments, and even the rabbits which had been slain. The rabbits they cast away among the soapweed plants that grew on the slope at the foot of the cliff. The garments they spread out on the snow, and by their knowledge cleansed and made them perfect, even more perfect than they had been before.

Then, flinging the huge body of the giant Demon down into the depths of the canyon, they turned them about, and calling out gentle words to the maiden, entered and restored her. And she, seeing in them not their usual ugly persons, but handsome youths (as like to one another as are two deer born of the same mother), was greatly comforted; and bending low, and breathing upon their hands, thanked them over and over for the rescue they had brought her. But she crouched herself low with shame that her garments were but few. When, behold! the youths went out and brought in to her the garments they had cleaned by their knowledge, restoring them to her.

Then, spreading their mantles by the door of the cave, they slept there that night, in order to protect the maiden, and on the morrow wakened her. They told her many things, and showed her many things which she had not known before, and counseled her thus, "It is not fearful that a maiden should marry; therefore, O maiden, return unto thy people in the Village of the Gateway of the River of Zuñi. This morning we will slay rabbits unnumbered for you, and start you on your way, guarding you down the snow-covered valley; and when you are in sight of your home we will leave you, telling you our names."

So, early in the morning the two gods went forth; and flinging their sticks among the soapweed plants, behold! as though the soapweed plants were rabbits, so many lay killed on the snow before these mighty hunters. And they gathered together great numbers of these rabbits, a string for each one of the party. And when the sun had risen clearer in the sky, and his light sparkled on the snow around them, they took the rabbits to the maiden and presented them, saying, "We will carry each one of us a string of these rabbits." Then taking her hand, they led her out of the cave and down the valley, until, beyond on the high black mesas at the Gateway of the River of Zuñi, she saw the smoke rise from the houses of her village. Then turned the two War-gods to her, and they told her their names. And again she bent low, and breathed on their hands. Then, dropping the strings of rabbits which they had carried close beside the maiden, they swiftly disappeared.

Thinking much of all she had learned, she continued her way to the home of her father and mother. And as she went into the town, staggering under her load of rabbits, the young men and the old men and women and children beheld her with wonder; and no hunter in that town thought of comparing himself with the Maiden Huntress of Kyawana Tehua-tsana. The old man and the old woman, who had mourned the night through and sat up anxiously watching, were overcome with happiness when they saw their daughter returning; and as she laid the rabbits at their feet, she said, "My father and my mother, foolish have I been, and much danger have I passed through. But two wondrous youths have taught me that a woman may be a huntress and yet never leave her own fireside. I will marry, when some good youth comes to me, and he will hunt rabbits and deer for me, for my parents and my children."

The White Stone Canoe

There was once a very beautiful girl, who died suddenly on the day she was to have been married to a handsome young man. He was also brave, but his heart was not proof against this loss. From the hour she was buried, there was no more joy or peace for him. He went often to visit the spot where the women had buried her, and sat musing there, when it was thought by some of his friends he would have done better to try to amuse himself in the chase, or by diverting his thoughts on the warpath. But war and hunting had both lost their charms for him. His heart was already dead within him. He pushed aside both his war club and his bow and arrows.

He heard the old people say that there was a path that led to the land of souls, and he determined to follow it. He accordingly set out one morning, after having completed his preparations for the journey. At first he hardly knew which way to go. He was only guided by the tradition that he must go south.

For a while he could see no change in the face of the country. Forests, and hills, and valleys, and streams had the same look they wore in his native place. There was snow on the ground when he set out, and it was sometimes seen to be piled and matted on the thick trees and bushes. At length it began to diminish, and finally disappeared. The forest assumed a more cheerful appearance, and the leaves put forth their buds, and before he was

96

aware of the completeness of the change, he found himself surrounded by spring. He had left behind him the land
of snow and ice.

The air became mild; the dark clouds of winter had
rolled away from the sky. A pure field of blue was above
him, and as he went he saw flowers beside the path, and
heard the songs of birds. By these signs he knew that he
was going the right way, for they agreed with the tradi-
tions of his tribe. At length he spied a path. It led him
through a grove, then up a long and elevated ridge, on the
very top of which he came to a lodge. At the door stood
an old man with white hair, whose eyes, though deeply
sunk, had a fiery brilliancy. He had a long robe of skins
thrown loosely around his shoulders and a staff in his
hands. It was Chebiabos.

The young Chippewa began to tell his story, but the
venerable chief stopped him before he had spoken ten
words. "I have expected you," he replied, "and had just
risen to bid you welcome to my abode. She whom you
seek passed here but a few days since, and being fatigued
with her journey, rested herself here. Enter my lodge
and be seated, and I will then satisfy your inquiries,
and give you directions for your journey from this point."
Having done this, they both went to the lodge door. "You
see yonder gulf," said he, "and the wide stretching blue
plains beyond. It is the land of souls. You stand upon
its borders, and my lodge is the gate of entrance. But
you cannot take your body along. Leave it here with your
bow and arrows, your bundle, and your dog. You will find
them safe on your return."

So saying, he re-entered the lodge, and the freed traveler bounded forward, as if his feet had suddenly been
given wings. But all things retained their natural colors
and shapes. The woods and leaves, and streams and
lakes, were only brighter and more beautiful than he had
ever seen. Animals bounded across his path, with a free-
dom and a confidence which seemed to tell him there was
no bloodshed here. Birds of beautiful plumage inhabited

the groves, and sported in the waters. There was but one thing in which he saw a very unusual effect. He noticed that his passage was not stopped by trees or other objects. He appeared to walk directly through them. They were, in fact, but the souls or shadows of material trees. He became sensible that he was in a land of shadows.

When he had traveled half a day's journey through a country which was continually becoming more attractive, he came to the banks of a broad lake, in the center of which was a large and beautiful island. He found a canoe of shining white stone tied to the shore. He was now sure that he had come the right path, for the aged man had told him of this. There were also shining paddles. He immediately entered the canoe, and took the paddles in his hands, when to his joy and surprise, on turning round, he beheld the object of his search in another canoe, exactly its counterpart in everything. She had exactly imitated his motions, and they were side by side.

They at once pushed out from shore and began to cross the lake. Its waves seemed to be rising, and at a distance looked ready to swallow them up; but just as they entered the whitened edge of them they seemed to melt away, as if they were but the images of waves. But no sooner was one wreath of foam passed, than another, more threatening still, rose up. Thus they were in perpetual fear; and what added to it, was the clearness of the water, through which they could see many beings who had perished before, and whose bones lay strewed on the bottom of the lake. The Master of Life had, however, decreed to let them pass, for the actions of neither of them had been bad. But they saw many others struggling and sinking in the waves. Old men and young men, males and females of all ages and ranks were there; some passed, and some sank. It was only the little children whose canoes seemed to meet no waves.

At length, every difficulty was gone, as in a moment, and they both leaped out on the happy island. They felt that the very air was food. It strengthened and nourished them. They wandered together over the blissful fields, where everything was formed to please the eye and the ear. There were no tempests—there was no ice, no chilly winds—no one shivered for the want of warm clothes; no one suffered hunger; no one mourned the dead. They saw no graves. They heard of no wars. There was no hunting of animals, for the air itself was their food.

Gladly would the young warrior have remained there forever, but he was obliged to go back for his body. He did not see the Master of Life, but he heard his voice in a soft breeze. "Go back," said this voice, "to the land from whence you come. Your time has not yet come. The duties for which I made you, and which you are to perform, are not yet finished. Return to your people and accomplish the duties of a good man. You will be the ruler of your tribe for many days. The rules you must observe will be told you by my messenger, who keeps the gate. When he surrenders back your body, he will tell you what to do. Listen to him, and you shall afterward rejoin the spirit which you must now leave behind. She is accepted, and will be ever here, as young and as happy as she was when I first called her from the land of snows."

When this voice ceased, the young man awoke. It all had been a dream.

The Moose Wife

A young man living with his mother concluded to go into the forest to hunt for a whole year, collecting and drying meat, and intending at the end of that period to return to visit his mother. So he traveled a long way into the forest to a region in which he thought there was plenty of deer and other game. There, having built a cabin, he began housekeeping by himself. His daily routine was to make a fire, get breakfast, and then start off to hunt. He would stay away hunting all day. Often when he got home at night he was so tired that he would not take the trouble to prepare supper, but throwing himself on his couch, he would go to sleep. He was collecting a great quantity of cured meat.

One evening when he was returning from a long tramp, he saw, as he neared his cabin, smoke issuing from the smoke hole in the roof. At this he became greatly troubled, for he thought that the fire may have spread and ignited his lodge. Running into the lodge as quickly as possible, what was his surprise to find a bright fire burning in the fire pit, and his kettle, which had been suffered to boil, hanging on the crook in such a way as to keep its contents hot. He wondered who had come to cook for him, for during the time he had lived there and during his journeys he had never found a cabin, nor had he seen a human being. He searched all around to see whether he could find a trace of a person's visit.

100

He saw that the deer he had brought home the evening before was dressed and hung up, that a pile of wood that he had cut had been brought in, that everything had been put in order, and that even corn bread had been made. On the way home he had thought of going to bed the moment he set foot in the cabin, so he was greatly rejoiced to find a warm supper awaiting him. He sat down and ate the supper, thinking to himself, "Surely the person who got this ready will come back," but no one came.

The next morning he started as usual to hunt. When he returned in the evening, he looked to see whether smoke was coming out of the smoke hole of his cabin. There was smoke issuing from it, and again he found supper ready for him. On discovering a partially finished braid of fibers of bark, he knew that a woman had been at work. He saw, moreover, that she had also put a large number of his green deerskins to soak, preparatory to making buckskin. Thereupon he thought how good she was, and he resolved to see her, whoever she might be, even if he had to give up hunting in order to do so.

In the morning he started off as though he were going to hunt, but went only a short way into the woods to a place whence he could watch the cabin. He had built no fire that morning, so that he might be able to tell the moment smoke began to rise from the lodge. Stealthily creeping back toward his home, he soon saw smoke rising from the cabin. As he drew nearer, he saw what to him was a woman come out of the lodge and take up an armful of wood.

When she went into the lodge, he followed her as quickly as possible. There he found a beautiful young woman, to whom he said, "You have been very kind to me, and I am very thankful to you." She said in reply, "I knew you were starving for lack of a woman's aid, so I came to see whether you would take me as your wife." He accepted her offer, for he was very happy that she was willing to remain. She never left him after that. Every day she tanned the deerskins and cooked for him, working hard all the time. His wife was beautiful, and he loved her dearly.

Before the end of a year, a boy was born to them, and they were perfectly happy. When the time was near to fulfill his promise to visit his mother, she said to him, "I know you promised to visit your mother, and the time is now here. I have everything ready for you. I have made moccasins for you and for your mother." He said in reply, "I wonder how I can carry her some meat, for she lives a long way off." "You have only to choose the meat you want," she replied; "I know how you can carry it." He decided to take some of every kind.

She warned him to be true and faithful to her while away, for many women when they saw what a good hunter he was would ask him of his mother. She said, "You must be true to me as I will be to you. You must never yield to temptation, for I shall know if you do, and you will never see me again." He promised her everything she asked. Early the next morning she asked him to go to the river with her; it was not far from the cabin. She knew how he came, and that he would reach his mother's home sooner by going on the river. When they reached the bank, she took out of her bosom a tiny canoe. He wondered what she was going to do with so little a plaything. She told him to take hold of one end and to pull away from her. On doing so, the canoe stretched out until it was a very large one.

Then they brought on their backs basketful after basketful of meat, which they packed away in the canoe. Giving him a package, she said, "I have made these moccasins for your mother. Here is another package for you. I wish you to put on a pair every morning, throwing away the old ones."

He promised to return in the fall, and then they parted. When he reached his mother's lodge, the news spread that a certain woman's son had returned after a year's hunting, and many came to see him and the great amount of meat he had brought. He did not tell even his mother that he was married, and many young girls asked for him as a husband. His mother had a beautiful girl in view for him, and continually urged him to marry her, but he would not consent. After a while he said to his mother, "I am going to the woods again. I have a cabin there, and sometime you will know why I do not wish to marry." So saying, he started off.

When he reached the river, he shook his boat as his wife had instructed him to do, whereupon it again stretched out. Getting aboard, he started up the river. When he neared his cabin, he saw his wife waiting for him and his little boy running around at play, and they were very happy again. She told him she loved him better than ever, for he had withstood temptation.

Another year passed. They had all the meat they could take care of, and another boy had been born to them. Again she got him ready to carry meat to his mother, just as she had done before. She seemed, however, to feel that this time he would yield to temptation, so she said to him, "If you marry another woman, you will never see me again; but if you love me and your children, you will be true to us and come back. If you are not true, I will not be surprised if your new wife will soon be sucking her moccasins from hunger, for your *orenda,* your magic power for hunting, will vanish." He promised her everything.

As before, on reaching home his fame as a hunter brought many beautiful girls to ask for him in marriage. Again his mother urged him to marry, and the temptation to yield then was far greater than the first time, but he resisted and was ready to start for his cabin, when one day a beautiful stranger, appearing in the village, came to his mother's lodge. The mother urged him to marry her, as she was so lovely, and he finally yielded.

The wife in the woods, knowing the conditions, said, "Now children, we must be getting ready to go away. Your father does not love us and will never come back to us." Though the children were troubled by their mother's tears, still they were full of play and fun, but the poor mother was always weeping while preparing to leave her home.

After the man had taken a second wife, the meat in his

lodge began to fall away strangely. He could almost see it disappear, though there was a good supply when he married. In a few days but little was left. He went hunting but could kill nothing; he went day after day, but always had the same ill luck, for he had lost his magic power for hunting, as his wife had foretold. One day when he came home from hunting, he found his new wife sucking her moccasin, for she was famishing from hunger. He cried and sobbed, saying, "This is my punishment; she warned me that this would happen if I was untrue to her." Thereupon he decided to go back to his first wife and children at once and never to leave them again.

He set out without saying a word to the starving wife or his anxious mother. When he reached his cabin not a single footprint was to be seen. He went in, but only to find it empty—wife and children were not there, nor any meat, but their worn moccasins were hanging up. The sight of these made him very sad. As he was nearly starved, he searched everywhere for food. On the hearth he found three small mounds of ashes, of different sizes, the third being very small. Sitting down, he wondered what this could mean, for he knew that it must have been left by his wife as a sign to him should he ever come to the cabin. At last he made up his mind that he had three children now, and he determined to find them even if he had to follow them to the end of the world.

He mused, "My boys are very playful, and as they followed their mother they must have hacked the trees as they went." Indeed, as the mother and the boys were starting away, the boys said, "We will make some sign, so that if our father ever thinks of us and comes back, he will be able to follow us." But the mother said, "No, children, you must not; he will never come, for he has another wife, and will never think of his children in the woods." Nevertheless, as they went on and played by the way, the boys hacked the trees and shot arrows in sport, so the father was soon able to trace them. He found that after a day's journey they had camped for the night, for he discovered the remains of a fire, and on a tree near by, four pairs of worn-out moccasins. Tying these in a bundle, he hung it on his arm.

Again he walked all day, finally coming to the remains of a fire, near which he saw four pairs of worn moccasins hanging up as before. He was very tired and hungry.

The next morning he traveled on, and as before, found the remains of a fire and four pairs of worn moccasins hanging on a tree. He always took these with him. Near noon the next day he saw smoke in the distance, seeming to rise from a cabin, and so it proved to be. He saw also two boys playing around, running, and shooting arrows; on seeing him they ran to tell their mother that a man was coming. On looking out, she recognized her husband, whereupon she told the boys to stay inside the lodge. He had not recognized the children as his sons, but supposed they belonged to the people living in the cabin.

As he was very hungry and tired, he thought he would go in and ask for food. The woman turned her back as he entered, but the eldest boy, recognizing his father, ran to him and put his hand on his knee. The father, however, not recognizing the child, gently pushed his hand away. At this moment the mother, turning around, saw this action. "There," she said, "I told you to keep away from him, for he does not love you."

Now the man, recognizing his wife, cried out, begging her to forgive him and to receive him home again. He seemed to be sorry, and begged so hard that she forgave him and brought him his little daughter, born after he had gone away. Ever afterward he was true to his Moose wife (for she was a Moose woman), and never again left his home in the woods. He and his little family were always very happy.

The Origin of Strawberries

When the first man was created and a mate was given to him, they lived together very happily for a time, but then began to quarrel, until at last the woman left her husband and started off toward Nundagunyi, the Sun land, in the east. The man followed alone and grieving, but the woman kept on steadily ahead and never looked behind, until Unelanunhi, the great Apportioner, the Sun, took pity on him and asked him if he was still angry with his wife. He said he was not, and Unelanunhi then asked him if he would like to have her back again, to which he eagerly answered, "Yes."

So Unelanunhi caused a patch of the finest ripe huckleberries to spring up along the path in front of the woman, but she passed by without paying any attention to them. Farther on he put a clump of blackberries, but these also she refused to notice.

Other fruits, one, two, and three, and then some trees covered with beautiful red service berries, were placed beside the path to tempt her, but she still went on, until suddenly she saw in front a patch of large ripe strawberries, the first ever known.

She stooped to gather a few to eat, and as she picked them she chanced to turn her face to the west, and at once the memory of her husband came back to her, and she found herself unable to go on. She sat down, but the longer she waited, the stronger became her desire for her husband, and at last she gathered a bunch of the finest berries and started back along the path to give them to him. He met her kindly and they went home together.

The Maiden of the Yellow Rocks

In the days of the ancients, when our ancestors lived in the Village of the Yellow Rocks, also in the Salt City, also in the Village of the Winds, and also in the Village of the White Flowering Herbs, and also in the Village of Odd Waters, where they come forth, when in fact all these broken-down villages were inhabited by our ancients, there lived in the Village of the Yellow Rocks a very beautiful maiden, the daughter of the high priest.

Although a woman, she was wonderfully endowed by birth with the magic knowledge of the hunt and with the knowledge of all the animals who contribute to the sustenance of man—game animals. And, although a woman, she was also somewhat bad in her disposition, and selfish, in that, possessing this knowledge above all other men and women, she concluded she would have all these animals—the deer, antelope, rabbits—to herself.

So, through her wonderful knowledge of their habits and language, she communicated with them and charmed them, and on the top of the mountain—where you will see to this day the ancient figures of the deer cut in the rock—she built a huge corral, and gathered one after another all the deer and antelope and other wild animals of that great country. And the hunters of these villages hunted in vain. They trailed the deer and the antelope, but they lost their trails and always came home with nothing save the weapons they took with them. But this maiden, whenever

107

she wished for deer, would go to her corral and kill whatever animal she wanted. So she and her family always had plenty of meat, while others were without it; always had plenty of buckskins with which to make moccasins and apparel, while others were every day wearing out their old supply and never able to replenish it.

Now, this girl was surpassingly beautiful, and was looked upon by many a young man as the flower of his heart and the one on whom he would ultimately concentrate his thoughts for life. Among these young men, the first to manifest his feelings was a youth from the Village of the Winds.

One day he said to his old people, "I am going courting." And they observed that he made up a bundle of various precious things for women's dress and ornamentation— necklaces, snow-white buckskin moccasins and leggings, and embroidered skirts and mantles—and, taking his bundle on his shoulders, he started off for the Village of the Yellow Rocks.

When he reached the village he knew the home of the maiden by the beauty of the house. Among other houses it was alone of its kind. Attached to the ladder was the crosspiece carved as it is in these days, but hanging from it was a fringe of black hair with which they still ornament certain houses when they have sacred ceremonies; and among this fringe were hung hollow stalactites from a sacred cave on the Colorado Chiquito, which sounded, when the wind blew them together, like little bells. This fringe was full of them, so that when a stranger came to this important chief priest's house he no sooner touched the ladder rung at the foot than the bells tinkled, and they knew someone was coming.

As he placed his foot on the lowermost rung of the ladder, *chi-la-li* sang the bells at the top.

Said the people within, "Someone is coming."

Step after step he went up, and still the bells made music at the top, and as he stepped over on the roof, *thud, thud,* his footsteps sounded as he walked along; and when he reached the door, those within said, "Thou comest?" And he replied, "I come. Draw me in"; by which expression he meant that he had brought with him a present to the family. Whenever a man has a bundle to hand down, it is the place of the woman to take it; and that is called "drawing a man in," though she only takes his bundle, and he follows. In this case he said, "Draw me in," and the maiden came to the top of the ladder and took the bundle and dropped it on the floor. They knew by the appearance of the bundle what the object of the visit was.

The old man was sitting by the fireplace—it was nighttime—and as the stranger entered, said, "Thou hast come?"

The young man answered, "Yes."

Said the old man, "It is not customary for a stranger to visit the house of a stranger without saying something of what may be in his thoughts."

"It is quite true," said the youth; "I come thinking of this maiden, your daughter. It has occurred to me that I might happily and without fear rest my thoughts and hopes on her; therefore I come."

The daughter brought forth food for the young man and bade him eat. He reached forth his hand and partook of the food. She sat down and took a mouthful or two, whereby they knew she was favorably disposed. She was favorably disposed to all appearance, but not in reality. When he had finished eating, she said, "As you like, my father. You are my father." She answered to her own thoughts, "Yes, you have often reproached me for not treating with more gentleness those who come courting me."

Finally said the father, "I give ye my blessing and sacred speech, my children. I will adopt thee as my child."

"My children," said the father, after a while, when he had smoked a little, "the stranger, now a son, has come a long distance and must be weary."

So the maiden led him to an upper chamber, and said, "Rest here; you are not yet my husband. I would try you in the morning. Get up early, when the deer are most plentiful, and go forth and slay me a fine one, and then indeed shall we rest our hopes and thoughts on each other for life."

"It is well," said the youth; and he retired to sleep, and in the morning arose early. The maidens gave into his hands the food for the day; he caught up his bows and arrows and went forth into the forest and mountains, seeking for the deer. He found a superb track and followed it until it suddenly disappeared, and though he worked hard and followed it over and over again, he could find nothing.

While the young man was out hunting and following the tracks for nothing, the young girl went out, so as to be quite sure that none of her deer should get out. And what did she do? She went into the river and followed it against the current, through the water beyond the village and where the marked rocks stand, up the canyon to the place where her deer were gathered. They were all there, peaceful and contented. But there were no tracks of the girl; no one could follow where she went.

The young man hunted and hunted, and at nighttime, all tired out and hungry, took his way back to the home of the maiden. She was there.

"Ha!" said she, "what good fortune today?"

And the young man with his face dragged down and his eyes not bright, answered, "I found no game today."

"Well," said the girl, "it is too bad; but under the circumstances we cannot rest our thoughts and hopes on each other for life."

"No, I suppose not," said the young man.

"Here is your bundle," said the girl. She raised it very carefully and handed it to him. He took it over his shoulder, and after all his weary work went on his way home.

The very next day a young man named Halona, when he heard of this, said, "Ha! ha! What a fool he was! He didn't take her enough presents; he didn't please her. I am said to be a very pleasant fellow" (he was a very conceited

young man); "I will take her a bundle that will make things all right."

So he put into a bundle everything that a woman could reasonably want—for he was a wealthy young man, and his bundle was very heavy—put on his best dress, and with fine paint on his face started for the home of the maiden. Finally, his foot touched the lowermost rung of the ladder; the stalactites went on jingling above as mounted, and *thud* went his bundle as he dropped it on the roof.

"Somebody has come," said the people below. "Listen to that!"

The maiden shrugged her shoulders and said, "Thou comest?"

"Yes," answered the young man, "draw me in."

So she reached up and pulled the huge bundle down into the room, placing it on the floor, and the young man followed it down.

Said the old man, who was sitting by the fire, for it was night, "Thou comest. Not thinking of nothing doth one stranger come to the house of another. What may be thy thoughts?"

The young man looked at the maiden and said to himself, "What a magnificent creature she is! She will be my wife, no fear that she will not." Then said he aloud, "I came, thinking of your daughter. I would rest my hopes and thoughts on her."

"It is well," said the old man. "It is the custom of our people and of all people, that they may possess dignity, that they may be the heads of households; therefore, young men and maidens marry and establish themselves in certain houses. I have no objection. What dost thou think, my daughter?"

"I have no objection," said the daughter.

"Ah, what did I tell you?" said the youth to himself, and ate with a great deal of satisfaction the meal placed before him.

The father laid out the cornhusks and tobacco, and

they had a smoke. Then he said to his daughter, "The stranger who is now my son has come a long way, and should not be kept sitting up so long."

As the daughter led him to another room, he thought, "What a gentle creature she is! How softly she steps up the ladder."

When the door was reached, she said, "Here we will say good night."

"What is the matter?" he asked.

Said she: "I would like to know of my husband this much, that he is a good hunter; that I may have plenty of food all my days, and plenty of buckskins for my clothing. Therefore I must ask that in the morning you go forth and hunt the deer, or bring home an antelope for me."

The young man quickly recovered himself, and said," It is well," and lay himself down to rest.

So the next morning he went out, and there was the maiden at the top of the house watching him. He couldn't wait for daylight; he wanted the Sun, his father, to rise before his time, and when the Sun did rise he jumped out of bed, tied his quiver to his belt, took his bow in his hand, and with a little luncheon the maiden had prepared for him, started off.

As he went down the river he saw the maiden was watching him from the top of the house. So he started forward and ran until he was out of sight, to show how fine a runner he was and how good a hunter, because he was reputed to be a very strong and active young man. He hunted and hunted, but did not find any deer, nor even any tracks.

Meanwhile, the maiden went up the stream as before and kept watch of the corral; and he fared as the other young man had fared. At night he came home, not quite so downcast as the other had been, because he was a young man of more self-reliance.

She asked him, as she met him, "Haven't you got any deer today?"

He answered, "No."

She said, "I am sorry, but under the circumstances, I don't see how we can become husband and wife."

So he carried his bundle home.

The next day there was a young man in the City of Salt who heard of this; not all of it, but he heard that day after day young men were going to the home of this maiden to court her, and she turned them all away. He said, "I dare say they didn't take enough with them." So he made up two bundles and went to the home of the maiden, and he said to himself, "This time it will be all right."

When he arrived, much the same conversation was gone through as before with the other young men, and the girl said, when she lighted him to the door of his room, "My young friend, if you will find a deer for me tomorrow, I will become your wife and rest my hope only on you."

"Mercy on me!" thought the young man to himself, "I have always been called a poor hunter. What shall I do?"

The next morning he tried, but with the same results.

Now, this girl was keeping the deer and antelope and other animals so long closed up in the corral that the people in all the villages round about were ready to die of hunger for meat. Still, for her own gratification she would keep these animals shut up.

The young man came back at evening, and she asked him if he had found a deer for her.

"No," said he. "I could not even find the trail of one."

"Well," she said, "I am sorry, for your bundles are heavy."

He took them up and went home with them.

Finally, this matter became so much talked about that the two small gods on the top of Thunder Mountain, who lived with their grandmother where our sacrificial altar now stands, said, "There is something wrong here; we will go and court this maiden." Now, these gods were extremely ugly in appearance when they chose to be— mere pigmies who never grew to man's stature. They were always boys in appearance, and their grandmother was always crusty with them; but they concluded one night that they would go the next day to woo this maiden.

Said one to the other, "Suppose we go and try our luck with her." Said he, "When I look at you, you are extremely handsome."

Said the other to him, "When I look at you, you are extremely handsome."

They were the ugliest beings in human form, but in reality were among the most magnificent of men, having power to take any form they chose.

Said the elder one, "Grandmother, you know how much talk there is about this maiden in the Village of the Yellow Rocks. We have decided to go and court her."

"You miserable, dirty, ugly little wretches! The idea of your going to court this maiden when she has refused the finest young men in the land!"

"Well, we will go," said he.

"I don't want you to go," replied she. "Your names will be in the mouths of everybody; you will be laughed and jeered at."

"We will go," said they. And without paying the slightest attention to their grandmother, they made up their bundle—a very miserable bundle it was. The younger brother put in little rocks and sticks and bits of buckskins and all sorts of worthless things, and they started off.

"What are you carrying this bundle for?" asked Ahaiyuta, the elder brother.

"I am taking it as a present to the maiden," said Matsailema, the younger one.

"She doesn't want any such trash as that," said the other. "They have taken very valuable presents to her before; we have nothing to take equal to what has been carried to her by others."

They decided to throw the bundle away altogether, and started out with absolutely nothing but their bows and arrows.

As they proceeded they began to kill wood rats, and continued until they had slaughtered a large number and had a long string of them held up by their tails.

"There!" exclaimed the younger brother. "There is a fine present for the girl." They knew perfectly well how things were, and were looking out for the interests of their children in the villages round about.

"Oh, my younger brother!" said the elder. "These will not be acceptable to the girl at all; she would not have them in the house!"

"Oh, yes, she would," said the younger. "We will take them along as a present to her."

So they went on, and it was hardly noon when they arrived with their strings of rats at the white cliffs on the southern side of the canyon opposite the village where the maiden lived.

"Here, let us sit down in the shade of this cliff," said the elder brother, "for it is not proper to go courting until evening."

"Oh, no," said the younger, "let us go along now. I am in a hurry! I am in a hurry!"

"You are a fool!" said the elder brother. "You should not think of going courting before evening. Stay here patiently."

So they sat down in the shade of the cliff. But the younger kept jumping up and running out to see how the sun was all the afternoon, and he would go and smooth out his string of rats from time to time, and then go and look at the sun again. Finally, when the sun was almost set, he called out, "Now, come on!"

"Wait until it is wholly dark," said the other. "You never did have any patience, sense, or dignity about you."

"Why not go now?" asked the younger.

So they kept quarreling, but the elder brother's wish prevailed until it was nearly dark, when they went on.

The elder brother began to get very bashful as they approached the village. "I wonder which house it is," said he.

"The one with the tallest ladder in front of it, of course," said the other.

Then the elder brother said in a low voice, "Now, do behave yourself; be dignified."

"All right!" replied the younger.

When they got to the ladder, the elder one said in a whisper, "I don't want to go up here; I don't want to go courting; let's go back."

"Go along up," said the younger.

"Keep still; be quiet!" said the elder one. "Be dignified!"

They went up the ladder very carefully, so that there was not a tinkle from the bells.

The elder brother hesitated, while the younger one went on to the top, and over the edge of the house.

"Now!" cried he.

"Keep still!" whispered the other; and he gave the ladder a little shake as he went, and the bells tinkled at the top.

The people downstairs said, "Who in the world is coming now?"

When they were both on the roof, the elder brother said, "You go down first."

"I will do nothing of the kind," said the other, "you are the elder."

The people downstairs called out, "Who comes there?"

"See what you have done, you simpleton!" said the elder brother. Then with a great deal of dignity he walked down the ladder. The younger one came tumbling down, carrying his string of rats.

"Throw it out, you fool; they don't want rats!" said the elder one.

"Yes, they do," replied the other. "The girl will want these; maybe she will marry us on account of them!"

The elder brother was terribly disturbed, but the other brought his rats in and laid them in the middle of the floor.

The father looked up, and said, "You come?"

"Yes," said the two odd ones.

"Sit down," said the old man. So they sat down, and food was placed before them.

"It seems," said the father, "that ye have met with luck today in hunting," as he cast his eyes on the string of rats.

"Yes," said the two.

So the old priest went and got some prayer meal, and, turning the faces of the rats toward the east, said a short prayer.

"What did I tell you?" said the younger brother. "They like the presents we have brought. Just see!"

Presently the old man said, "It is not customary for strangers to come to a house without something in mind."

"Quite so," said the younger brother.

"Yes, my father," said the elder one, "we have come thinking of your daughter. We understand that she has been wooed by various young men, and it has occurred to us that they did not bring the right kind of presents."

"So we brought these," said the younger brother.

"It is well," said the old man. "It is the custom for maidens and youths to marry. It rests with my daughter."

So he referred the matter to his daughter, and she said, "As you think, my father. Which one?"

"Oh, take us both!" said the younger brother.

This was rather embarrassing to the maiden, but she knew she had a safe retreat. So when the father admonished her that it was time to lead the two young men up into the room where the others had been placed, she told them the same story.

They said, "It is well."

They lay down, but instead of sleeping spent most of the night speculating as to the future.

"What a magnificent wife we will have," said one to the other.

"Don't talk so loud; everyone will hear you; you will be covered with shame!"

After a while they went to sleep, but were awake early the next morning. The younger brother began to talk to the elder one, who said, "Keep quiet; the people are not awake; don't disturb them!"

The younger one said, "The sun is rising."

"Keep quiet," said the other, "and when they are awake they will give us some luncheon to take with us."

But the younger one jumped up and went rushing about the house, calling out, "The sun is rising. Get up!"

The luncheon was provided, and when they started off the maiden went out on the housetop and asked them which direction they would take.

Said they, "We will go over to the south and will get a deer before long, although we are very small and may not meet with very good luck."

So they descended the ladder, and the maiden said to herself, "Ugly, miserable little wretches; I will teach them to come courting me this way!"

The brothers went off to the cliffs, and while pretending to be hunting, they ran back through the thickets near the house and waited to see what the maiden would do.

Pretty soon she came out. They watched her and saw that she went down the valley and presently ran into the river, leaving no trail behind, and took her course up the stream. They ran on ahead, and long before she had ascended the river found the path leading out of it up the mountain. Following this path, they came to the corral, and looking over it, they saw thousands of deer, mountain sheep, antelope, and other animals wandering around in the enclosure.

"Ha, here is the place!" the younger brother exclaimed. "Let us go at them now!"

"Keep quiet! Be patient! Wait till the maiden comes," said the elder one. "If we should happen to kill one of these deer before she comes, perhaps she has some magic power or knowledge by which she would deprive us of the fruits of our efforts."

"No, let us kill one now," said the other. But the elder one kept him curbed until the maiden was climbing the cliff, when he could restrain him no longer, and the youth pulled out his bow and let fly an arrow at the largest deer. One arrow, and the deer fell to the ground. And when the maiden appeared on the spot the deer was lying dead not far away.

The brothers said, "You come, do you? And here we are!"

She looked at them, and her heart went down and became as heavy as a stone, and she did not answer.

"I say, you come!" said the younger brother. "You come, do you?"

She said, "Yes." Then she said to herself, "Well, I suppose I shall have to submit, as I made the arrangement myself." Then she looked up and said, "I see you have killed a deer."

"Yes, we killed one; didn't have any difficulty at all," said the younger brother. "Come and help us skin him; we are so little and hungry and tired we can't do it. Come on."

So the girl went slowly forward, and in a dejected way helped them skin the deer. Then they began to shoot more deer, and attempted to drag them out; but the men were so small they could not do it, and the girl had to help them. Then they cut up the meat and made it into bundles. She made a large one for herself, and they made two little ones for themselves.

"Now," said they, wiping their brows, "we have done a good day's work, haven't we?" and they looked at the maiden with twinkling eyes.

"Yes," said she; "you are great hunters."

"Shall we go toward home?" asked the younger brother of the maiden. "It would be a shame for you to take such a bundle as that. I will take it for you."

"You little conceited wretch!" cried the elder brother. "Haven't I tried to restrain you? And now you are going to bury yourself under a bundle of meat!"

"No," said the younger brother, "I can carry it."

So they propped the great bundle of meat against a tree. The elder brother called on the maiden to help him; the younger one stooped down and received it on his back. They had no sooner let go of it than it fell on the ground and completely flattened the little man out.

"Mercy! Mercy! I am dying; help me out of here!" cried he.

So they managed to roll the thing off, and he got up and rubbed his back, complaining bitterly (he was only making believe), and said, "I shall have to take my little bundle."

So he shouldered his little bundle, and the maiden took the large one; but before she started she turned to the animals and said, "Oh, my children! these many days, throwing the warm light of your favor upon me, you have rested contented to remain away from the sight of men. Now, hereafter you shall go forth whithersoever you will, that the earth may be covered with your offspring, and men may once more have of your flesh to eat and of your pelts to wear." And away went the antelope, the deer, the mountain sheep, the elk, and the buffalo over all the land.

Then the young gods of war turned to the maiden and said, "Now, shall we go home?"

"Yes," said she.

"Well, I will take the lead," said the younger brother.

"Get behind where you belong," said the other; "I will precede the party." So the elder brother went first, the maiden came next, and the younger brother followed behind, with his little bag of meat.

So they went home, and the maiden placed the meat to dry in the upper rooms of the house.

While she was doing this, it was yet early in the day. The two brothers were sitting together, and whispering, "And what will she say for herself now?"

"I don't see what she can say for herself."

"Of course, nothing can she say for herself."

And when the meat was all packed away in the house and the sun had set, they sat by themselves talking this over, "What can she say for herself?"

"Nothing whatever; nothing remains to be done."

"That is quite so," said they, as they went in to the evening meal and sat with the family to eat it.

Finally the maiden said, "With all your hunting and the labors of the day, you must be very weary. Where you slept last night you will find a resting place. Go and rest yourselves. I cannot consent to marry you, because you have not yet shown yourselves capable of taking care of and dressing the buckskins, as well as of killing deer and antelope and such animals. For a long time buckskins have been accumulating in the upper room. I have no brothers to soften and scrape them; therefore, if you two will take the hair off all my buckskins tomorrow before sunset, and scrape the underside so that they will be thin and soft, I will consent to be the wife of one of you, or both."

And they said, "Oh, mercy, it is too bad!"

"We can never do it," said the younger brother.

"I don't suppose we can; but we can try," said the elder. So they lay down.

"Let us take things in time," said the elder one, after he had thought of it. And they jumped up and called to the maiden, "Where are those buckskins?"

"They are in the upper room," said she.

She showed them the way to the upper room. It was packed to the rafters with buckskins. They began to make big bales of these and then took them down to the river. When they got them all down there they said, "How in the world can we scrape so many skins? There are more here than we can clean in a year."

"I will tell you what," said the younger brother; "we will stow away some in the crevices of the rocks, and get rid of them in that way."

"Always hasty, always hasty," said the elder. "Do you suppose that woman put those skins away without counting every one of them? We can't do that."

They spread them out in the water that they might soak all night, and built a little dam so they would not float away. While they were thus engaged they heard someone talking, so they pricked up their ears to listen.

Now, the hill that stands by the side across from the Village of the Yellow Rocks was, and still is, a favorite home of the field mice. They are very prolific, and have to provide great bundles of wool for their families. But in the days of the ancients they were terrible gamblers and were all the time betting away their nests, and the young mice being perfectly bare, with no wool on them at all, died of cold. And still they kept on betting, making little figures of nests and betting these away against the time when they should have more. It was these mice which the two gods overheard.

Said the younger brother, "Listen to that! Who is talking?"

"Someone is betting. Let us go nearer."

They went across the river and listened, and heard the tiny little voices calling out and shouting.

"Let us go in," said the younger brother. And he placed his foot in the hole and descended, followed by the other. They found there an enormous village of field mice in human form, their clothes, in the shape of mice, hanging over the sides of the house. Some had their clothing all off down to their waists, and were betting as hard as they could and talking with one another.

As soon as the two brothers entered, they said, "Who comes?"

The two answered, "We come."

"Come in, come in," cried the mice; they were not very polite. "Sit down and have a game. We have not anything to bet just now, but if you trust us we will bet with you."

"What had you in mind in coming?" said an old field mouse with a broken tail.

They answered that they had come because they heard voices. Then they told their story.

"What is this you have to do?" asked the mice.

"To clean all the hair off those pelts tomorrow."

The mice looked around at one another; their eyes fairly sparkled and burned.

"Now then, we will help you if you will promise us something," said they; "but we want your solemn promise."

"What is that?" asked the brothers.

"That you will give us all the hair."

"Oh, yes," said the brothers; "we will be glad to get rid of it."

"All right," said they; "where are the skins?" Then they all began to pour out of the place, and they were so numerous that it was like water, when the rain is falling hard, running over a rock.

When they had all run out, the two War-gods drew the skins on the bank, and the field mice went to nibbling the hair and cleaning off the underside. They made up little bundles of the flesh from the skins for their food, and great parcels of the hair. Finally they said, "May we have them all?"

"No," said the brothers, "we must have eight reserved, four for each, so that we will be hard at work all day tomorrow."

"Well," said the mice, "we can't consent to leaving even so many, unless you promise that you will gather up all the hair and put it somewhere so that we can get it."

The two promised that, and said, "Be sure to leave eight skins, will you? And we will go to bed and rest ourselves."

"All right, all right!" responded the field mice.

So the brothers climbed up the hill to the town, and up the ladder, and slept in their room.

The next morning the girl said, "Now, remember, you will have to clean every skin and make it soft and white."

So they went down to the river and started to work. The girl had said to them that at midday she would go down and see how they were getting along. They were at work nearly all the forenoon on the skins. While the elder brother shaved the hair off, the younger one scraped them thin and softened them.

When the maiden came at noon, she said, "How are you getting along?"

"We have finished four and are at work on the fifth."

"Remember," said she, "you must finish all of them today, or I shall have to send you home."

So they worked away until a little before the sun set, when she appeared again. They had just finished the last. The field mice had carefully dressed all the others (they did it better than the men), and there they spread out on the sands like a great field of something growing, only white.

When the maiden came down she was perfectly overcome; she looked and looked and counted and recounted.

She found them all there. Then she got a long pole and fished in the water, but there were none.

Said she, "Yes, you shall be my husbands; I shall have to submit."

She went home with them, and for a long time they all lived together, the woman with her two husbands. They managed to get along very comfortably, and the two brothers didn't quarrel any more than they had done before.

Finally, there were born little twin boys, exactly like their fathers, who were also twins, although one was called the elder and the other the younger.

After a time the younger brother said, "Now, let us go home to our grandmother. People always go home to their own houses and take their families with them."

"No," said the elder one, "you must remember that we have been only pretending to be human beings. It would not do to take the maiden home with us."

"Yes," said the other, "I want her to go with us. Our grandmother kept making fun of us; called us little, miserable, wretched creatures. I want to show her that we amount to something!"

The elder brother could not get the younger one to leave the wife behind, and like a dutiful wife she said, "I will go with you." They made up their bundles and started out. It was a very hot day, and when they had climbed nearly to the top of Thunder Mountain, the younger brother said, "Ahem! I am tired. Let us sit down and rest."

"It will not do," said the elder brother. "You know very well it will not do to sit down; our father, the Sun, has forbidden that we should be among mortals. It will not do."

"Oh, yes, it will; we must sit down here," said the younger brother. And again his wish prevailed and they sat down.

At midday the Sun stood still in the sky, and looked down and saw this beautiful woman, and by the power of his withdrawing rays quickly snatched her from them while they were sitting there talking, she carrying her little children.

The brothers looked around and said, "Where is our wife?"

"Ah, there she is," cried the younger. "I will shoot her."

"Shoot your wife!" cried the elder brother. "No, let her go! Serves you right!"

"No," said the younger, "I will shoot her!" He looked up and drew his arrow, and as his aim was absolutely unerring, *swish* went the arrow directly to her, and she was killed. The power of life by which the Sun was drawing her up was gone, the thread was cut, and she fell over and over and struck the earth.

The two little children were so very small, and their bones so soft, that the fall did not hurt them much. They fell on the soft bank, and rolled and rolled down the hill, and the younger brother ran forward and caught them up in his arms, crying, "Oh, my little children!" and brought them to the elder brother, who said, "Now, what can be done with these little babies, with no mother, no food?"

"We will take them home to grandmother," said the younger brother.

"Our grandmother cannot take care of these babies," said the elder brother.

"Yes, she can, of course," said the younger brother. "Come on, come on! I didn't want to lose my wife and children, too; I thought I must still have the children; that is the reason why I shot her."

So one of them took one of the children, and the other one took the other, and they carried them up to the top of Thunder Mountain.

"Now then," said the elder brother, "we went off to marry; we come home with no wife and two little children, and with nothing to feed them."

"Oh, grandmother!" called out the younger brother.

The old woman hadn't heard them for many a day, for many a month, even for years. She looked out and said,

"My grandchildren are coming," and she called to them, "I am so glad you have come!"

"Here, see what we have," said the younger brother. "Here are your grandchildren. Come and take them!"

"Oh, you miserable boy, you are always doing something foolish. Where is your wife?" asked the grandmother.

"Oh, I shot her!" was the response.

"Why did you do that?"

"I didn't want my father, the Sun, to take them away with my wife. I knew you would not care anything about my wife, but I knew you would be very fond of the grandchildren. Here they are."

But she wouldn't look at all. So the younger brother drew his face down, and taking the poor little children in his arms said, "You unnatural grandmother, you! Here are two nice little grandchildren for you!"

She said, "How shall I feed them? Or what shall I do with them?"

He replied, "Oh, take care of them, take care of them!"

She took a good look at them, and became a true grandmother. She ran and clasped the little ones, crying out, "Let me take you away from these miserable children of mine!" She made some beds of sand for them, as Zuñi mothers do today, got some soft skins for them to lie on, and fed them with a kind of milk made of corn toasted and ground and mixed with water, so that they gradually enlarged and grew up to be nice children.

The Story of Mimkudawogoosk, Moosewood Man

Away in the woods dwelt a young woman alone. As she had no comrade, she was obliged to depend upon her own exertions for everything; she procured her own fuel, hunted and prepared her own food; she was often lonely and sad. One day, when gathering fuel, she cut and prepared a *noosagun*—poker for the fire—of *mimkudawok,* and brought it home with her; she did not bring it into the wigwam, but stuck it up in the ground outside. Some time in the evening she heard a sound, as of a human voice outside complaining of the cold, "*Numees kaooche*—My sister, I am cold." "Come in and warm yourself, then," was the answer. "I cannot come in; I am naked," was the reply. "Wait, then, and I will put you out some clothes," she replied. This was soon done.

He donned the robes tossed out to him, and walked in— a fine-looking fellow, who took his seat as the girl's younger brother; the poker which she left standing outside the door had been thus metamorphosed, and proved a very beneficial acquisition. He was very affable and kind, and withal an expert hunter; so that all the wants of the house were bountifully supplied. He was named Mimkudawogoosk, from the moosewood tree from which he sprang.

After a time his female friend hinted to him that it would

be well for him to seek a companion. "I am lonely," said she, "when you are away; I want you to fetch me a sister-in-law." To this reasonable suggestion he consented; and they talked the matter over and made arrangements for carrying their plans into execution. His sister told him where to go, and how to pass certain dangers.

"You will have to pass several nests of serpents; but you must not fight them nor meddle with them. Clap one end of your bow on the ground, and use it as a pole to assist you in jumping, and leap right straight across them."

Having received these instructions, he started on his journey. After a while his sister became lonely from the loss of his company, and resolved to follow him. To give him warning, she sang; he heard, and answered her in the same style, instructing her to go back and not come after him. She did so.

He went on till he came to a large Indian village. He followed his sister's instruction, and entered one of the meanest wigwams. There, as he expected, he found quite a bevy of pretty girls. The youngest of the group excelled in beauty; he walked up and took his seat by her side. As she remained seated, and the parents showed their acquiescence by their silence, this settled the matter and consummated the marriage. The beauty of his countenance and his manly bearing had won the heart of the maiden and the esteem of the father. But the young men of the village were indignant. The young lady had had many suitors, who had all been rejected; and now to have her so easily won by a stranger was outrageous. They determined to kill him.

Meanwhile his father-in-law told him to go out and try his hand at hunting, and when he returned successful they would prepare a festival in honor of the marriage. So he took his wife with him in his father-in-law's canoe, and following the directions given by the old man, pushed up the river to the hunting grounds, where he landed and constructed a temporary hut. He went into the hunting business in earnest. He was at home in that occupation; and before many days he had collected a large amount of fur and venison, and was prepared to return.

But a conspiracy had been formed to cut him off and rob him of his prize. A band of young men of the village, who were skilled in magical arts, had followed him and reached the place where he had pitched his hut. But now the trouble was how to proceed; they dared not attack him openly, and in wiles he might be able to outdo them. But they adopted this plan. One of them was to transform himself into a mouse, and insinuate himself under the blanket while the man was asleep, and then give him a fatal stab. But our hero was wide-awake. When the mouse approached, he quietly clapped his knee on him, all unconsciously, as he pretended, and squeezed the little fellow most lovingly.

The poor little mouse could not stand the pressure, and sang out most lustily. This aroused the wife, who, perceiving that her husband was resting his leg heavily upon some poor fellow, jogged him and tried to make him understand what was going on. But he was wonderfully dull of apprehension, and could not understand what she was saying, and managed by what seemed an all-unconscious movement to squeeze the wily foe, the small mouse, more affectionately. He did not design to kill him, however, but to frighten him and send him off. Finally he released him, and never did poor mouse make greater speed to escape. He carried the warning to his companions, and they concluded to beat a hasty retreat.

Mimkudawogoosk now prepared to return. He asked his wife if she was willing to take the canoe, with its load, back to the village alone, and allow him to go and fetch his sister; she said she was willing, and he saw her safely off. She arrived in due time, and made report to her father. All were amazed at the amount of fur and food collected in so short a time. They conveyed it all safely up to the village, and then awaited the return of the husband. After a few days he came, bringing his sister, and the feasts and sports began.

After racing and other sports, he was challenged to dive and see who could remain the longer under water. He accepted the challenge, and went out with his antagonist. "What are you?" said Mimkudawogoosk. "I am a loon," answered the other proudly; "but you—what are you?" "I am a Chigumooeech." "Ah!" Down went the divers; and after a long time the poor loon floated up to the top, and drifted dead down the river. The spectators waited a long while; and finally the Chigumooeech came up, flapped his wings exultingly, and came to land in triumph.

"Let us try a game of growing," said another. "What will you choose to be?" said Mimkudawogoosk. "I will be a pine tree," answered the other. "Very well, I am the elm," answered his rival. So at it they went. The one rose as a large white pine, encumbered with branches, which exposed him to the blasts of the hurricane. The other rose high, and naked of limbs; and when the blast came he swayed and bent, but retained his hold on the earth, while his rival was overturned and killed.

The stranger came off victorious in all the contests, and returned exulting to camp. The father-in-law was pleased and proud of him; but his other daughters—and especially the oldest—were dying of envy and rage, and the young men of the village were indignant.

Meanwhile our hero was presented by his wife with a fine little boy, and the oldest sister pretended to be very friendly, and asked permission to nurse the child. But the mother declined the offered assistance; she was suspicious of the barely hidden jealousy of her sister. "I can take care of my babe myself," she told her.

After a while the father-in-law advised Mimkudawogoosk to move back to his native place. The jealousy of the hunters was deepening. They were enraged to find themselves outdone, and their glory eclipsed in everything; they decided soon to make an attempt to rid themselves of him. He took the advice, and departed. His father-in-law provided him with a canoe and weapons, and bade him defend himself if attacked. He went, taking with him his wife, child, and sister. He had not gone far before he was pursued and overtaken. But he was found to be as good in battle as in the chase; his foes were soon killed or dispersed, and he and his family peacefully went on their way to their own land.

The Rabbit Goes Duck Hunting

The Rabbit was so boastful that he would claim to do whatever he saw anyone else do, and so tricky that he could usually make the other animals believe it all. Once he pretended that he could swim in the water and eat fish just as the Otter did, and when the others told him to prove it, he fixed up a plan so that the Otter himself was deceived.

Soon afterward they met again and the Otter said, "I eat ducks sometimes." Said the Rabbit, "Well, I eat ducks too." The Otter challenged him to try it; so they went up along the river until they saw several ducks in the water and managed to get near without being seen. The Rabbit told the Otter to go first. The Otter never hesitated, but dived from the bank and swam under water until he reached the ducks, when he pulled one down without being noticed by the others, and came back in the same way.

While the Otter had been under the water, the Rabbit had peeled some bark from a sapling and made himself a noose. "Now," he said, "just watch me." And he dived in and swam a little way under the water until he was nearly choking and had to come up to the top to breathe. He went under again and came up again a little nearer to the ducks. He took another breath and dived under, and this time he came up among the ducks and threw the noose over the head of one and caught it. The duck struggled hard and finally spread its wings and flew up from the water with the Rabbit hanging onto the noose.

It flew on and on until at last the Rabbit could not hold on any longer, but had to let go and drop. As it happened, he fell into a tall, hollow sycamore stump without any hole at the bottom to get out from, and there he stayed until he was so hungry that he had to eat his own fur, as the rabbit does ever since when he is starving. After several days, when he was very weak with hunger, he heard children playing outside around the trees. He began to sing:

> Cut a door and look at me;
> I'm the prettiest thing you ever did see.

The children ran home and told their father, who came and began to cut a hole in the tree. As he chopped away, the Rabbit inside kept singing, "Cut it larger, so you can see me better; I'm so pretty." They made the hole larger, and then the Rabbit told them to stand back so that they could take a good look as he came out. They stood away back, and the Rabbit watched his chance and jumped out and got away.

The Coyote

Once upon a time, Too-whay-shur-wee-deh, the Little Blue Fox, was wandering near a pueblo, and chanced to come to the threshing floors, where a great many crows were hopping. Just then the Coyote passed, very hungry, and while yet far off, said, "*Ai!* how the stomach cries! I will just eat Little Blue Fox." And coming, he said, "Now, Little Blue Fox, you have troubled me enough! You are the cause of my being chased by the dogs and people, and now I will pay you. I am going to eat you up this very now!"

"No, Coyote friend," answered the Little Blue Fox, "don't eat me up! I am here guarding these chickens, for there is a wedding in yonder house, which is my master's, and these chickens are for the wedding dinner. Soon they will come for the chickens, and will invite me to the dinner—and you can come also."

"Well," said the Coyote, "if that is so, I will not eat you, but will help you watch the chickens." So he lay down beside him.

At this, Little Blue Fox was troubled, thinking how to get away; and at last he said, "Friend Coyote, I make strange that they have not before now come for the chickens. Perhaps they have forgotten. The best way is for me to go to the house and see what the servants are doing."

"It is well," said the Coyote. "Go, and I will guard the chickens for you."

So the Little Blue Fox started toward the house; but

getting behind a small hill, he ran away with fast feet. When it was a good while, and he did not come back, the Coyote thought, "While he is gone, I will give myself some of the chickens." Crawling upon his belly to the threshing floor, he gave a great leap. But the chickens were only crows, and they flew away. Then he began to say evil of the Little Blue Fox for giving him a trick, and started on the trail, vowing, "I will eat him up wherever I catch him."

After many miles he overtook the Little Blue Fox, and with a bad face said, "Here! Now I am going to eat you up!"

The other made as if greatly excited, and answered, "No, friend Coyote! Do you not hear the *tombe*?" The Coyote listened, and heard a drum in the pueblo.

"Well," said the Little Blue Fox, "I am called for that dance, and very soon they will come for me. Won't you go too?"

"If that is so, I will not eat you, but we will go to the dance." And the Coyote sat down and began to comb his hair and to make himself pretty with face paint. When no one came, the Little Blue Fox said, "Friend Coyote, I make strange that the *alguazil*—officer—does not come. It is best for me to go up on this hill, whence I can see into the village. You wait here."

"He will not dare to give me another trick," thought the Coyote. So he replied, "It is well. But do not forget to call me."

So the Little Blue Fox went up the hill; and as soon as he was out of sight, he began to run for his life. Very long the Coyote waited; and at last, being tired, went up on the hill, but there was no one there. Then he was very angry, and said, "I will follow him, and eat him surely! Nothing shall save him!" And finding the trail, he began to follow as fast as a bird.

Just as the Little Blue Fox came to some high cliffs, he looked back and saw the Coyote coming over a hill. So he stood up on his hind feet and put his forepaws up against the cliff, and made many groans, and was as if much excited. In a moment came the Coyote, very angry, crying,

"Now you shall not escape me! I am going to eat you up now—now!"

"Oh, no, friend Coyote!" said the other; "for I saw this cliff falling down, and ran to hold it up. If I let go, it will fall and kill us both. But come, help me to hold it."

Then the Coyote stood up and pushed against the cliff with his forepaws, very hard, and there they stood side by side.

Time passing so, the Little Blue Fox said, "Friend Coyote, it is long that I am holding up the cliff, and I am very tired and thirsty. You are fresher. So you hold up the cliff while I go and hunt water for us both, for soon you too will be thirsty. There is a lake somewhere on the other side of this mountain. I will find it and get a drink, and then come back and hold up the cliff while you go."

The Coyote agreed, and the Little Blue Fox ran away over the mountain till he came to the lake, just as the moon was rising.

But soon the Coyote was very tired and thirsty, for he held up the cliff with all his might. At last he said, "*Ai!* how hard it is! I am so thirsty that I will go to the lake, even if I die!"

So he began to let go of the cliff, slowly, slowly, until he held it only with his fingernails; and then he made a great jump away backward, and ran as hard as he could to a hill. But when he looked around and saw that the cliff did not fall, he was very angry, and swore to eat Too-whay-shur-wee-deh the very minute he should catch him.

Running on the trail, he came to the lake, and there the Little Blue Fox was lying on the bank, whining as if greatly excited. "Now I will eat you up this minute!" cried the Coyote. But the other said, "No, friend Coyote! Don't eat me up! I am waiting for someone who can swim as well as you can. I just bought a big cheese from a shepherd to share with you, but when I went to drink, it slipped out of my hands into the water. Come here, and I will show you." He took the Coyote to the edge of the high bank, and pointed to the moon in the water.

"M—m!" said the Coyote, who was fainting with hunger. "But how shall I get it? It is very deep in the water, and I shall float up before I can dive to it."

"That is true, friend," said the other. "There is but one way. We must tie some stones to your neck, to make you heavy, so you can go down to it."

So they hunted about until they found a buckskin thong and some large stones; and the Little Blue Fox tied the stones to the Coyote's neck, the Coyote holding his chin up to help.

"Now, friend Coyote, come here to the edge of the bank and stand ready. I will take you by the back and count *weem, wee-si, pah-chu!* And when I say three, you must jump in and I will push—for now you are very heavy."

So he took the Coyote by the back of the neck, swaying him back and forth as he counted. And at *"pah-chu!"* he pushed hard, and the Coyote jumped and went into deep water, and never came out again!

Raven Pretends to Build a Canoe

After Raven had visited every country, he found a little hut in which were two women—a widow and her daughter; and the widow was very kind to him, and fed him with many kinds of food. After Raven had eaten, he said to the widow, "I will marry your daughter," and the widow agreed. Then Raven was glad that the widow's daughter was to marry him, for the widow's house was full of all kinds of food. The young woman who was the wife of Raven was very beautiful.

After a while Raven said to his young wife, "Now, my dear, you know that I love you very much, and therefore I shall build a nice little canoe for your mother. I shall go away tomorrow to look for red cedar. Then I will build a canoe for her. I want you to get ready, for I want to start early in the morning." The young woman repeated this to her mother.

Early the next morning the mother-in-law arose and prepared breakfast for her son-in-law. When it was ready she called her son-in-law. Raven arose and ate his breakfast. Then he went off to search for red cedar. He came back before it was evening, went to his wife, and told her that he had found a very good red cedar of proper size. He said, "I will cut it down tomorrow. Then I will cut it the right length for a canoe." His mother-in-law prepared supper for him, and she cooked all the food she had. After he had eaten his meal, he lay down; and while he was lying

138

there, he whispered to his wife, "When the canoe is finished, I will go around the island. You shall sit in the stern, your mother shall sit in the middle of the canoe, and I will sit in the bow. Then we shall have a happy time." Thus spoke Raven to his wife. Next morning he arose, while his mother-in-law prepared his breakfast.

After he had taken his meal, he took his mother-in-law's stone tools and went; and his mother-in-law and his wife heard him cut the tree with his stone axe. They also heard the large cedar tree fall, and after a while they heard also how he was working with the stone axe. He came home before it was evening, weary and sore on account of the hard work that he had been doing all day long. When he came home, he said to his wife, "Just tell your mother that I want her to boil for me a good dried salmon every evening, for I like the soup of dried salmon. It is very good for a man who is building a canoe." She did so every evening. When the fourth day came, Raven told his wife that the canoe was almost finished. By this time his mother-in-law's provisions were nearly spent, and some of her food boxes were empty.

A few days later Raven started again, and on the following morning he went to take along some food for his dinner. Now, the widow said to her daughter, "Go, my dear daughter, and see how long it may take until your husband has finished the canoe that he is building, but go secretly." Then the daughter went to the place where her husband was working. Unseen she arrived at the place where he was, and saw him standing at the end of an old rotten cedar tree, beating it with a stone axe to make a noise like a man who is working with an axe. His wife saw that there was a large hole in the rotten cedar tree, and therefore it made much noise when Raven was striking it. His wife left.

When she came to her mother, she told her all about her husband. Therefore they took the canoe and moved to their tribe. They took away all the provisions that were left. Raven went back before it was evening. Before he reached his mother-in-law's hut he was glad and whistled, because he thought his mother-in-law had prepared his supper for him. But when he went in, he saw that everything was gone. Nothing remained except empty boxes and a little fire. Then he was hungry again.

Manstin, the Rabbit

Manstin was an adventurous brave, but very kindhearted. Stamping a moccasined foot as he drew on his buckskin leggings, he said, "Grandmother, beware of Iktomi! Do not let him lure you into some cunning trap. I am going to the North Country on a long hunt."

With these words of caution to the bent old rabbit grandmother with whom he had lived since he was a tiny babe, Manstin started off toward the north. He was scarce over the great high hills when he heard the shrieking of a human child.

"*Wan!*" he said, pointing his long ears toward the direction of the sound; "*Wan!* That is the work of cruel Double-Face. Shameless coward! He delights in torturing helpless creatures!"

Muttering indistinct words, Manstin ran up the last hill and lo! in the ravine beyond stood the terrible monster with a face in front and one in the back of his head!

This brown giant was without clothes save for a wild-cat skin about his loins. With a wicked gleaming eye, he watched the little black-haired baby he held in his strong arm. In a laughing voice he hummed an Indian mother's lullaby, "*A-boo! Aboo!*" and at the same time he switched the naked baby with a thorny wild-rose bush.

Quickly Manstin jumped behind a large sage bush on the brow of the hill. He bent his bow, and the sinewy string twanged. Now an arrow stuck above the ear of Double-Face. It was a poisoned arrow, and the giant fell dead. Then Manstin took the little brown baby and hurried away from the ravine. Soon he came to a teepee from whence loud wailing voices broke. It was the teepee of the stolen baby, and the mourners were its heart-broken parents.

When gallant Manstin returned the child to the eager arms of the mother, there came a sudden terror into the eyes of both the Dakotas. They feared lest it was Double-Face come in a new guise to torture them. The rabbit understood their fear and said, "I am Manstin, the kindhearted—Manstin, the noted huntsman. I am your friend. Do not fear."

That night a strange thing happened. While the father and mother slept, Manstin took the wee baby. With his feet placed gently yet firmly upon the tiny toes of the little child, he drew upward by each small hand the sleeping child till he was a full-grown man. With a forefinger he traced a slit in the upper lip, and when on the morrow the man and woman awoke, they could not distinguish their own son from Manstin, so much alike were the braves.

"Henceforth we are friends, to help each other," said Manstin, shaking a right hand in farewell. "The earth is our common ear, to carry from its uttermost extremes one's slightest wish for the other!"

"*Ho!* Be it so!" answered the newly made man.

Upon leaving his friend, Manstin hurried away toward the North country whither he was bound for a long hunt. Suddenly he came upon the edge of a wide brook. His alert eye caught sight of a rawhide rope staked to the water's brink, which led away toward a small round hut in the distance. The ground was trodden into a deep groove beneath the loosely drawn rawhide rope.

"*Hun-he!*" exclaimed Manstin, bending over the freshly made footprints in the moist bank of the brook. "A man's footprints!" he said to himself. "A blind man lives in yonder hut! This rope is his guide by which he comes for his daily water!" surmised Manstin, who knew all the peculiar contrivances of the people. At once his eyes became fixed upon the solitary dwelling, and hither he followed his curiosity—a real blind man's rope.

Quietly he lifted the door-flap and entered. An old toothless grandfather, blind and shaky with age, sat upon the ground. He was not deaf, however. He heard the entrance and felt the presence of some stranger.

"*How!* grandchild," he mumbled, for he was old enough to be grandparent to every living thing, "*how!* I cannot see you. Pray, speak your name!"

"Grandfather, I am Manstin," answered the rabbit, all the while looking with curious eyes about the wigwam.

"Grandfather, what is it so tightly packed in all these buckskin bags placed against the tent poles?" he asked.

"My grandchild, those are dried buffalo meat and venison. These are magic bags which never grow empty. I am blind and cannot go on a hunt. Hence a kind Maker has given me these magic bags of choicest foods."

Then the old, bent man pulled at a rope which lay by his right hand. "This leads me to the brook where I drink! And this," said he, turning to the one on his left, "and this takes me into the forest, where I feel about for dry sticks for my fire."

"Grandfather, I wish I lived in such sure luxury! I would lean back against a tent pole, and with crossed feet I would smoke sweet-willow bark the rest of my days," sighed Manstin.

"My grandchild, your eyes are your luxury! You would be unhappy without them!" the old man replied.

"Grandfather, I would give you my two eyes for your place!" cried Manstin.

"*How!* you have said it. Arise. Take out your eyes and give them to me. Henceforth you are at home here in my stead."

At once Manstin took out both his eyes, and the old man put them on! Rejoicing, the old man started away with his young eyes while the blind rabbit filled his dream pipe, leaning lazily against the tent pole. For a short time it was a most pleasant pastime to smoke willow bark and to eat from the magic bags.

Manstin grew thirsty, but there was no water in the small dwelling. Taking one of the rawhide ropes, he started toward the brook to quench his thirst. He was young and unwilling to trudge slowly in the old man's footpath. He was full of glee, for it had been many long moons since he had tasted such good food. Thus he skipped confidently along, jerking the old weather-beaten rawhide spasmodically, till all of a sudden it gave way and Manstin fell headlong into the water.

"En! En!" he grunted, kicking frantically amidstream. All along the slippery bank he vainly tried to climb, till at last he chanced upon the old stake and the deeply worn footpath. Exhausted and inwardly disgusted with his mishaps, he crawled more cautiously on all fours to his wigwam door.

Dripping with his recent plunge, he sat with chattering teeth within his unfired wigwam.

The sun had set and the night air was chilly, but there was no firewood in the dwelling. "Hin!" murmured Manstin and bravely tried the other rope. "I go for some firewood!" he said, following the rawhide rope which led into the forest. Soon he stumbled upon thickly strewn dry willow sticks. Eagerly with both hands he gathered the wood into his outspread blanket. Manstin was naturally an energetic fellow.

When he had a large heap, he tied two opposite ends of the blanket together and lifted the bundle of wood upon his back, but alas! he had unconsciously dropped the end of the rope, and now he was lost in the wood!

"Hin! hin!" he groaned. Then pausing a moment, he set his fanlike ears to catch any sound of approaching footsteps. There was none. Not even a night bird twittered to help him out of his predicament.

With a bold face, he made a start at random. He fell into some tangled wood where he was held fast. Manstin let go his bundle and began to lament having given away his two eyes.

"Friend, my friend, I have need of you! The old oak-tree grandfather has gone off with my eyes, and I am lost in the woods!" he cried with his lips close to the earth.

Scarcely had he spoken when the sound of voices was audible on the outer edge of the forest. Nearer and louder grew the voices: one was the clear flute notes of a young brave, and the other the tremulous squeaks of an old grandfather.

It was Manstin's friend with the Earth Ear and the old grandfather. "Here, Manstin, take back your eyes," said the old man, "I knew you would not be content in my stead, but I wanted you to learn your lesson. I have had pleasure seeing with your eyes and trying your bow and arrows, but since I am old and feeble I much prefer my own teepee and my magic bags!"

Thus talking, the three returned to the hut. The old grandfather crept into his wigwam, which is often mistaken for a mere oak tree by little Indian boys and girls.

Manstin, with his own bright eyes fitted into his head again, went on happily to hunt in the North country.

The Loon's Necklace

The Medicine Man was sad, and for good reason, as he sat facing the bright beams of the afternoon sun. A sky of shimmering turquoise crowned the fragrant forest. It was the Moon of Painted Leaves. The hardwoods were tinted with crimson, copper, orange-red, and tawny russet shades. The quivering leaves of the aspens shone like burnished gold, reflecting the mellow, golden light of the sun and the black spires of spruce and pine towered skyward, just beyond the village. Overhead, a golden eagle drifted in the cloudless sky, but the eyes of the medicine man did not follow the wonder of its effortless hovering. He felt the warm touch of autumn on his face. His keen ears heard the faintest rustle of the woodland wild folk, but he saw them not. Dark Night, the medicine man, was sorrowful because he was blind. As he sat in front of his lodge, he heard the voice of his scolding wife. She added to his troubles by her constant complaints.

"Why weave you not baskets or make arrows, like other men who live in the night shadows?" she grumbled. "If you did, we could trade such things for food and skins. Then we would not know hunger and cold, as we will when snow flies. People now pay you little for your counsel as a medicine man. They say that you only know things by fours and that four cannot be strong medicine, cannot cure their ills. All you can think of and say is 'four.' Our people laugh when you say, 'When the owl hoots four

146

times, seek spruce sap for your cough.' Or, 'Place four
white pebbles on the red rock by the lake shore on the
fourth day,'" she mocked cruelly.

Dark Night heard, but he was patient. "Four is my medicine sign," he told her. "I learned it in my dream when my
secret totem and medicine animal were revealed."

"Why call you not on your totem to help us now?"
demanded his wife.

"When the time comes, I will," he promised patiently.

Only when he heard the quavering laugh of a loon come
from a near-by lake did the sad, resigned look leave his
face. Then he would smile and listen, and his lips would
move in unspoken answers to the wild, weird calls.

The "painted leaves" fell. A wild wind blew from the
north. Winter came.

The fear of hunger flowed like mist in the hearts of the
people. A black cloud of dread hung over the lodges of the
tribe. Even before the Snow Moon, hunting had been bad.
With the snow it became worse. Bands of hunters
returned to the village with the same story: neither animals nor birds were to be found. Lone hunters, the best in
the tribe, brought back no game, even after long, cold
days on the trail. Then the chief sent his young men
through the deep snow to neighboring tribes with beads
and weapons to trade for food. They returned with the
same trade goods which they had taken with them. Their
friendly neighbors also sought food in vain. There was
none to spare. Then, when the Hunger Moon shone in the
sad sky, there was none at all.

One night of bitter cold, lying awake in his lodge, Dark
Night heard, four times, the wild, wavering, warning cry of
a loon directly overhead. Instantly he dozed and dreamed.
In his troubled sleep his mind's eye saw a vision of sickness, sorrow, famine, danger, and death. Throughout his
dream he heard always the unearthly, high-pitched, savage attack cry of wolves coming ever nearer. Four loud,
haunting loon laughs awoke him. Sleep suddenly left him,
but the dream stayed in his mind. The awful attack call of

the wolf packs and the four warning notes of the loon were still with him when night left to let daybreak come.

When the sun shone, he groped his way to the council lodge. Inside, the chief of the band sat with the tribal medicine man and the wisest men of the tribe. Dark Night stood before them. "This is how it will be," he warned them as he told of his dream and the coming attack by wolf packs in four days' time. Those in council silently mocked him.

"Were the shadow of hunger not in my heart, I would laugh," the tribal medicine man declared. The Wise Ones smiled pityingly but were silent.

When they heard of Dark Night's warning, the people of the village made fun of him. They had ceased to respect or fear his powers as a medicine man. They pointed their fingers at him and tried to forget their hunger in their silent mockery.

At the end of the fourth day, as night spread its dark, star-studded blanket over the village, the mockers heard the savage cry of wolves. Fear spread like fire in the hearts of the people. They were scared, silent, stunned, for fierce, starving wolf packs came. That night the ravenous beasts raided the village. They cruelly injured men and women and carried away children before they could be driven off with fire and weapons. Each night the bloodthirsty wolves attacked and killed, and for days the bravest warriors feared to leave the village.

Then the chief sent his tribal medicine man to Dark Night and begged him to go to the council lodge. At once he obeyed his chief and followed the well-beaten trail through the deep snow to the meeting place. This time the chief and his counselors did not mock Dark Night.

"Help us," pleaded the chief as he guided the blind medicine man to the place of honor beside him. "Tell us what to do. It has been whispered by the Wise One that you have a magic bow. Arrows fired from that bow, they tell, cannot miss. Let our best hunter use it, should the wolves come again tonight."

"No one but I can bend the magic bow," declared Dark Night, "but tonight I will use it if your young men will bring me many hunting arrows."

"You will have all of our best arrows," promised the chief. He gave orders that the warriors and young men take their finest arrows to the lodge of Dark Night at once. The wife of the medicine man received them. She was now proud of the blind husband she had mocked before the snow came.

That night the wolves attacked again. Dark Night, dressed in his best buckskin hunting dress, circled the village. He held his magic bow and was guided by a great warrior who carried many arrows but no bow. When Dark Night heard the movement of a wolf he quickly placed an arrow on the bow thong, pointed the shaft in the direction of the sinister sound and pulled the bow taut. As the song of the bow thong whipped the darkness, the whistle of feathered shaft was followed each time by the death howl of a wolf. The snarls of famished beasts shattered the silence of the night. With blazing eyes and bristling hackles, the wolves fought each other with blood-flecked jaws that they might devour the bodies of their fellows which had fallen to Dark Night's bow. Arrows, fired by a tireless arm, flew from the magic bow until the pale fingers of morning groped among the trunks of the gray birches. Then the wolves fled, leaving many great, gray bodies stretched out in the crimson-stained snow. The hungry people feasted on the slain beasts and presents were piled high before the lodge of Dark Night. Often from that night until the snows left to let spring come, the blind medicine man's bow twanged to serve his people. Then the grass came back, deer returned to the forests, and the people were happy again.

Late one sun-filled evening, Dark Night sat outside his fine new lodge which the grateful people had made for him. A smile hovered about his lips and he seemed to be listening. Clearly, loudly, from the distant lake came the strange, soul-stirring cry of a loon. Four times did the quavering *wah-hoo-o-o-o-o-o* blend with the serene spring song of the fragrant forest. Once again Dark Night dressed himself in his finest buckskin. Around his neck he reverently placed his most prized possession, a necklace made of gleaming, snow-white shells. Refusing the help of many willing hands, he groped his way from tree to tree toward the loon call and the lake. When the cry sounded directly in front of him, the medicine man held onto the slim trunk of a paper-birch tree while he thrust the toe of his moccasin-clad foot forward. It touched soft, saffron sand at the edge of the lake. The setting sun, which he could not see, was sinking in a flaming curtain of splendor on the placid water of the silver-misted lake. Startlingly the loon call broke the silence. Never before had Dark Night heard the notes so loud and clear and near. Tremblingly the medicine man spoke, "O Father Loon, my totem bird, I have a wish which my heart prays may be granted."

"Speak, my son, that I may know your desire," replied a deep, musical voice.

The words came from a point so close to Dark Night's feet that he was startled. He managed to murmur, "For many, many moons I have lived in a darkness deeper than darkest night. I pray you, let my eyes see the wonders which I can only sense."

"Faith makes you believe. Faith will make you see, my son. You have been patient. Climb onto my back and hold tight to my wings."

Astonishment, fear, eagerness and hope were strong in Dark Night's heart as he did as he was bid. He grasped the loon's wings firmly and the great bird dived. In the space of an indrawn breath, the medicine man felt the cold waters of the lake flow beneath his sightless eyes.

The loon came to the surface when the distant shore was reached. "Has the light come to your eyes, my son?"

"No, Father Loon, all is still dark."

"Hold tightly," warned the loon.

Once again it dived smoothly beneath the surface and

swam to the opposite shore. When they reached it, the loon asked the same question.

"Not yet, Father Loon, but I seem to see a grayness before me."

When the lake had been crossed for the third time, the loon again asked, "Has the light come?"

"Yes, Father Loon, I can now see, though but dimly."

Again the loon warned the medicine man to hold on. Then it dived. Again the water flowed swiftly against the open eyes of the medicine man.

When the loon asked the question for the fourth time, the medicine man stood on the spot from where he had first heard the loon's loud laugh. When he looked down, he clearly saw a great loon floating feather-light on the surface of the lake in front of him. Dark Night flung his arms upward, hands held high, in a heartfelt gesture of thanks.

"Father Loon," he gasped, and his voice was choked with joy and grateful tears, "I can see! How can I thank you? How can I ever repay you?" Then, swift as the swoop of a hawk, he knew. He would give the loon his greatest treasure, his sacred necklace. Fumbling fingers at last loosened the treasured collar. With both trembling hands outstretched, he dropped the band of glistening white shells over the loon's head. As it raised its neck, the glittering, snowy collar glided gently down its black feathers. Like a lovely necklace it shone on the bird's neck. Some shells fell from the collar and lay sparkling like snow crystals on the loon's dark back and wings. The bird raised its long black beak skyward. Four times its lilting laugh filled the luminous twilight with music of savage splendor.

The heart of the medicine man was glad when he saw that his lovely collar of shells had become a glistening feather necklace, white as feathery flakes of snow.

The Origin of the Medicine Society

There was in the old times a young chief who was a
hunter of great cunning, but though he killed many animals he never took advantage of their positions. He never
shot a swimming deer or a doe with a fawn, he never
killed an animal fatigued by a long run nor took one
unawares. Before the hunt he always threw tobacco and
made a ceremony to ask permission to kill game. Nor was
he ever ungrateful to the animals of the woods who had
been his friends for so many years. The flesh that was useless he left for the wolves and birds, calling to them as he
left it, "Come, my friends, I have made a feast for you."
Likewise when he took honey from a tree, he left a portion
for the bears, and when he had his corn harvested, he left
open ears in the field for the crows, that they might not
steal the corn sprouts at the next planting. He fed the fish
and water animals with entrails and offal. No ruthless
hunter was he but thoughtful. He threw tobacco for the
animals in the woods and water, and made incense for
them with the *oyenkwaonwe*, the sacred tobacco, and
threw it even for the trees.

He was a well-loved chief, for he remembered his friends
and gave them meat. All the animals were his friends, and
all his people were loyal to him. All this was because he
was good, and he was known as the "protector of the
birds and beasts." So he was called. It is supposed that his
own name was His-hand-is-red.

The southwest country is a land of mysteries. There are many unknown things in the mountains there and also in the waters. The wildest people have always lived there, and some were very wise and made different things. When, many years ago, the Ongwe honwe, the Iroquois, began to make excursions to this distant country they encountered many nations that were friendly and more that were hostile. The Iroquois used to like to go to this country for there they learned new things and found new plants and new kinds of corn and beans, and when they would fight and destroy a tribe they would carry away curiously made things and some captives back to their own country.

While one of these exploring parties was in the far southwest looking for war and new things, a band of very savage people attacked them. The young chief, the friend of the animals, was with the party, and being separated from the rest of his party, was struck down by a tomahawk blow. The enemy cut a circle around his scalp lock and tore it off. He could not fight strong because he was tired and very hungry from the long journey, so he was killed. The enemy knew him because he had been a brave fighter and killed a good many of their people in former battles, so they were glad when they killed him and prized his scalp. Now he lay dead in a thicket, and none of his warriors knew where he was, but the enemy showed them his scalp. So they knew he was dead, but they did not kill all the Iroquois.

Black night came and alone upon the red and yellow leaves the chief lay dead, and his blood was clotted upon the leaves where it had spilled. The night birds scented the blood and hovered over the body, the owl and the whippoorwill flew above it, and Oshadagea, the dew eagle, swooped down from the regions over the clouds. "He seems to be a friend," they said. "Who can this man be?" A wolf sniffed the air and thought he smelled food. Skulking through the trees he came upon the body, dead and scalped. His nose was upon the clotted blood, and he liked blood. Then he looked into the face of the dead man and leaped back with a long yelping howl—the dead man was the friend of the wolves and the animals and birds.

His howl was a signal call and brought all the animals of the big woods, and the birds dropped down around him. All the medicine animals came—the bear, the deer, the fox, the beaver, the otter, the turtle, and the big horned deer (moose). Now the birds around him were the owl, the whippoorwill, the crow, the buzzard, the swift hawk, the eagle, the snipe, the white heron, and also the great chief of all birds, Oshadagea, who is the eagle that flies in the world of our Creator above the clouds.

These are all the great medicine people, and they came in council about their killed friend. Then they said, "He must not be lost to us. We must restore him to life again." Then a bird said, "He is our friend, he always fed us. We cannot allow our friend to die. We must restore him." Then the wolf came up to the body and said, "Here is our friend, he always gave us food in time of famine. We called him our father, now we are orphans. It is our duty to give him life again. Let each one of us look in our medicine packets and take out the most potent ingredient. Then let us compound a medicine and give it." Then the owl said, "A living man must have a scalp."

So the animals made a wonderful medicine, and in its preparation some gave their own lives and mixed them with the medicine roots. When the medicine was made, all of it was contained in the bowl of an acorn. So they poured it down the throat of the man, and the bear, feeling over the body, found a warm spot over his heart. Then the bear hugged him close in his hairy arms and kept him warm. The crow had flown away for the scalp but could not find it. Then the white heron went, but while flying over a bean field thought herself hungry and stopped to eat and when filled was too heavy to rise again. Then the pigeon hawk, the swiftest of the birds, said that he would go and surely find it.

By this time the enemy had become aware that the

animals were holding a council over their friend whom they had slain, and so they carefully guarded the scalp which they stretched upon a hoop and swung on a thong over the smoke hole of a lodge. The pigeon hawk, impatient at delay shot upward into the air and flying in wide circles discovered the scalp dangling over the fire drying in the hot smoke. Hovering over the lodge for a moment he dropped down, and snatching the scalp shot back upward into the clouds, faster and farther than the arrows that pursued him swift from the strong bows of the angered enemy. Back he flew, his speed undiminished by his long flight, and placed the scalp in the midst of the council. It was smoky and dried and would not fit the head of the man. Then big crow (buzzard) emptied his stomach on it to clean it of smoke and make it stick fast, and Oshadagea plucked a feather from his wing and dipped it in the pool of dew that rests in the hollow of his back and sprinkled the water upon it. The dew came down in round drops and refreshed the dry scalp as it does a withered leaf. The man had begun faintly to breathe when the animals placed the scalp back in his head, and they saw that truly he would revive. Then the man felt a warm liquid trickling down his throat, and with his eyes yet shut he began to talk the language of the birds and animals.

And they sang a wonderful song, and he listened and remembered every word of the song. This song the animals told him was the charm song of the medicine animals, and that when he wished the favor of the great medicine people, and when he felt grateful, to make a ceremony and sing the song. So also they told him that they had a dance and a dance song, and that they would teach him the dance. So they danced and some shook rattles made of the squashes (gourds), and though his eyes were closed he saw the dance and he knew all the tunes.

Then the animals told him to form a company of his friends and on certain occasions to sing and dance this ceremony, for it was a great power and called all the medicine animals together, and when the people were sick, they would devise a medicine for them. Now they said that he must not fail to perform the ceremony and throw tobacco for them. The name of the ceremony was *Hadidos*.

Then the chief asked the medicine people what the ingredients of the medicine were, and they promised to tell him. At a time the animals should choose they would notify him by the medicine song. Now, he could not receive the secret because he had been married. Only *hoyahdiwadoh*—virgin men—may receive the first knowledge of mysteries. Now, the chief greatly wished for the medicine, for he thought it would be a great charm and a cure for the wounds received in war. After a time the chief was lifted to his feet by the hand of the bear. Then he recovered his full life, and when he opened his eyes he found himself alone in the midst of a circle of tracks. He made his way back to his people and related his adventure. He gathered his warriors together and in a secret place sang the medicine song of the animals, the *Hadidos*. So they sang the song, and each had a song and they danced.

After some time, the chiefs decided to send another war party against the enemy in the southwest to punish the hostile people who were attacking them. Then the friend of the birds and animals said, "It is well that we destroy them for they are not a reasonable people," and so he went with his party.

Now after a certain number of days, the party stopped in an opening in the forest to replenish their stock of food. Now the place where they stopped was grassy and a good place for camp. Now a short distance away, a half day's journey, was a deer lick and near it a clear spring and a brook that ran from it, and to this place all the animals came to drink. The party wanted fresh meat and so dispatched two young men, *hoyahdiwadoh,* to the lick for game. As they approached it, they heard the sound of a distant song, and drawing near to the lick, they sat down on the bank over the spring and listened to the song. It was a most wonderful song and floated through the air to them. At a distance away, the animals came and drank, but so entranced were the young men by the music that they killed none. Through the entire night, they sat listening to the song, and learned sections of the song.

In the morning, they returned to the camp and reported what they had heard to their chief. Then said the chief, "That song is for the good of the medicine. You must find the source of the song and discover the medicine that will make us powerful in war and cure all our ills. You must purge yourselves and go again on the morrow." So the young men did as directed and went again to the spring and threw tobacco upon its surface. As night came on they listened, and again heard the great song. It was louder and more distinct than before. Then they heard a voice singing from the air and telling them the story of their lives and they marveled greatly. The song grew louder, and as they listened they discovered that it emanated from the summit of a mountain. So they returned in the morning and reported to their chief and sang to him parts of the song. Then he said, "You must cleanse yourselves again, and this time do not return until you have the medicine, the song, and the magic."

So the young men cleansed themselves again and went to the spring. As the thick night came on, they heard the singing voices clear and loud, ringing from the mountaintop. Then said one of the young men, "Let us follow the sound to its source," and they started in the darkness.

After a time they stumbled upon a windfall, a place where the trees had been blown down in a tangled mass. It was a difficult place to pass in the darkness, for they were often entrapped in the branches, but they persevered, and it seemed that someone was leading them. Beings seemed to be all about them, yet they could not see them, for it was dark. After they had extricated themselves from the windfall, they went into a morass, where their footsteps were guided by the unseen medicine animals.

Now the journey was a very tedious one, and they could see nothing. They approached a gulf and one said, "Let us

go up and down the gulf and try to cross it," and they did
and crossed one gulf. Soon they came to another, where
they heard the roaring of a cataract and the rushing of
waters. It was a terrifying place, and one of the young men
was almost afraid. They descended the slope and came to
a swift river. Its waters were very cold, but they plunged
in and would have been lost if someone unseen had not
guided them. So they crossed over, and on the other side
was a steep mountain which they must ascend, but could
not because it was too steep. Then one of the young
men said, "Let us wait here awhile and rest ourselves
for we may need our strength for greater dangers." So
he said. But the other said, "I am rested, we must go
onward somehow."

When he had so spoken, a light came flying over and
sang for them to follow it. So they followed the winged
light and ascended the mountain, and they were helped.
The winged light kept singing, "Follow me, follow me, follow me!" And they were safe when they followed and were
not afraid. Now the singing, flying beacon was the whippoorwill. He led them. After a time the light disappeared,
but they struggled up the mountainside unaided by its
guidance. The way became very stony, and it seemed that
no one was helping them now. Then they wished that
their unseen friends would help them, so they made a
prayer and threw sacred tobacco on the path. Then the
light came again, and it was brighter; it glowed like the
morning, and the way was lighted up. The singing continued all this while; they were nearing its source, and they
reached the top of the mountain.

They looked about for they heard the song near at
hand, but there was no one there. They saw nothing but a
great stalk of corn springing from a flat rock. Its four roots
stretched in the four directions, north, east, south, and
west. They listened and discovered that the music
emanated from the cornstalk. It was wonderful. The corn
was a mystically magic plant, and life was within it. Then
the winged light sang for them to cut the root and take a

piece for medicine. So they made a tobacco offering and cut the root. Red blood like human blood flowed out from the cut, and then the wound immediately healed. Then the unseen speaker said, "This root is a great medicine, and now we will reveal the secret of the medicine." So the voices told them the composition of the medicine that had healed the chief and instructed them how to use it. They taught the young men the *Ganota,* the medicine song that would make the medicine strong and preserve it. They said that, unless the song was sung, the medicine would become weak, and the animals would become angry because of the neglect of the ceremonies that honored their medicine. Therefore, the holders of the medicine must sing the all-night song for it. And they told them all the laws of the medicine, and the singing light guided them back to the spring, and it was morning then. The young men returned to their chief and told him the full story of their experiences, and he was glad for he said, "The medicine will heal all wounds."

It was true, the medicine healed the cuts and wounds made by arrows and knives, and not one of the Iroquois was killed in their battle with the enemy. When they returned home, the chief organized the lodges of the medicine and the medicine people, and the name of the society was *Hadidos.* The medicine was called *niganigaa*—little dose—because its dose was so small.

The Mouse's Children

Once, a long time ago, when the Cheyennes lived in earth houses, their village was on a stream, and the houses stood in a row along the bank. The camp was short of food and everyone was hungry, and all the people were going out to hunt buffalo. They started, but one young man did not leave with the others; he stayed in the camp for some time after they had gone. He had determined that he would be the last person to start.

At length he set out, and as he passed the houses, he heard in one of them a woman crying. He wondered who this could be, for everyone had left the village, and he stopped and listened. After he had listened for a little while, he determined that he would go over and see who it was that was crying. As he drew near the house, the mourning grew lower and lower, and when he reached the house the woman had stopped crying. He went to the door and looked in, and saw a woman sitting at the foot of a bed, and a man at the head of the bed. When he looked in the door the man spoke to him, greeting him, and said to the woman, "Get him something to eat." The young man sat down, and presently the woman put before him some dried meat and some marrow fat, and he ate.

After he had finished eating, the man said to the guest, "This woman, Mouse Woman, is crying and mourning because she has lost her children. They have been taken prisoner. She had her children in the arrow lodge, and they are there now and cannot get out." The man and the woman begged this young man to help get her children back. "For," said the man, "this woman has been crying ever since she lost her children."

The young man listened to all that they said, and at length he promised to try to do all he could to get her children back for her.

At last the sun began to get low in the west, and the young man stood up and said to these people, "Now I must go on and follow up the camp." The man said again to him, "The woman's children are in the medicine bundle in the lodge that you will find in the center of the camp. Do what you can to help her."

The young man said, "I will try in every way I can to get these children. If I can get them out tonight, I will come back at once, tonight."

He started on the trail of the camp, and traveled fast, but it was after night when he reached the camp. He had been thinking hard all the time as he traveled along, to see what he could do to get this woman's children. As he went along, he prepared presents, and as he came near to the arrow lodge, he began to mourn and to cry.

The arrow keeper in his lodge heard the sound of his mourning, and as it drew nearer he said to his wife, "Someone is coming with gifts; get all things ready and then go out." The woman got things ready, and when the young man came to the door of the lodge, she went out. The medicine man spoke, asking the young man to come in. He went in, and the host asked him to come over and sit by him at the back of the lodge.

"Why have you come to see me?" said the arrow keeper; and the young man told him that he had come to make these offerings. The medicine man took them and prayed over them, performing the needed ceremonies. Then he gave them back to the young man and told him to take them out in front of the lodge and spread them over the arrow bundle where it hung over the door.

When he went out to spread his gifts over the arrow

bundle, he thrust his hand into the bundle, and found there a mouse's nest with four little mice in it. After he had got the mice and put them in a fold of his robe, and had spread the gifts over the arrow bundle, he started back to the old village. When he had come within hearing distance of it, he could hear the woman still crying for her children. He kept on, and as he drew nearer the lodge, the mourning grew lower, and when he had come to the door it stopped.

He entered and said, "Well, I have brought you your children," and he handed her the little mice, and she and the man kissed the children. Then the man said to the young man, "You see how foolish my wife was to keep her children in the arrow lodge. They were lost, and she might never have seen them again, but you have helped her and brought them back to her. Now I will give you a name which shall become great, and which everyone shall hear of. You shall become a leading man, and always when people are talking of wars and fights your name shall be mentioned first. Your name shall be Mouse's Road."

After the man had talked in this way for a little time, the young man happened to look out of the door, and as he did so he heard the sound of mice squeaking and running, and looking back, he saw that the man and the woman had turned into mice and had run under the bed, and that he was there alone.

Now the young man returned to the camp, and as he followed the trail he was continually praying, for he remembered what the mouse person had told him. When he reached the camp, he went to his mother's lodge. She said to him, "Where have you been? I thought you would have been here long ago."

"No," he said, "I only just got in." Then said his mother, "A war party left while you were away. They sent for you to come with them." The young man said nothing, but the next morning he started and followed up the trail of the war party, and overtook them and went on with them.

In the first fight that they had, he, first of all, killed an enemy, and when he told what he had done, the people learned that his name was Mouse's Road. When the party got back, some old man cried out through the camp that Mouse's Road had killed the first enemy. In all fights after that, he was always the first to do some great thing, and his name was always mentioned first.

After this war party had returned, they counted many coups and had many scalp dances. Also, on the hunt they got many buffalo and dried much meat, and then they returned to their village.

The Theft from the Sun

Once Old Man was traveling around, when he came to the Sun's lodge, and the Sun asked him to stay a while. Old Man was very glad to do so.

One day the meat was all gone, and the Sun said, "*Kyi!* Old Man, what say you if we go and kill some deer?"

"You speak well," replied Old Man. "I like deer meat."

The Sun took down a bag and pulled out a beautiful pair of leggings. They were embroidered with porcupine quills and bright feathers. "These," said the Sun, "are my hunting leggings. They are great medicine. All I have to do is to put them on and walk around a patch of brush, when the leggings set it on fire and drive the deer out so that I can shoot them."

"Hai-yah!" exclaimed Old Man. "How wonderful!" He made up his mind he would have those leggings, if he had to steal them.

They went out to hunt, and the first patch of brush they came to, the Sun set on fire with his hunting leggings. A lot of white-tail deer ran out, and they each shot one.

That night, when they went to bed, the Sun pulled off his leggings and placed them to one side. Old Man saw where he put them, and in the middle of the night, when everyone was asleep, he stole them and went off. He traveled a long time, until he had gone far and was very tired, and then, making a pillow of the leggings, lay down and slept. In the morning, he heard someone talking. The Sun was saying, "Old Man, why are my leggings under your head?" He looked around, and saw he was in the Sun's lodge, and thought he must have wandered around and got lost, and returned there. Again the Sun spoke and said, "What are you doing with my leggings?" "Oh," replied Old Man, "I couldn't find anything for a pillow, so I just put these under my head."

Night came again, and again Old Man stole the leggings and ran off. This time he did not walk at all; he kept running until pretty near morning, and then lay down and slept. You see what a fool he was. He did not know that the whole world is the Sun's lodge. He did not know that, no matter how far he ran, he could not get out of the Sun's sight. When morning came, he found himself still in the Sun's lodge. But this time the Sun said, "Old Man, since you like my leggings so much, I will give them to you. Keep them." Then Old Man was very glad and went away.

One day his food was all gone, so he put on the medicine leggings and set fire to a piece of brush. He was just going to kill some deer that were running out, when he saw that the fire was getting close to him. He ran away as fast as he could, but the fire gained on him and began to burn his legs. His leggings were all on fire. He came to a river and jumped in. The burnt leggings fell away in pieces.

Perhaps the Sun did this to him because he tried to steal the leggings.

The Dun Horse

Many years ago, there lived in the Pawnee tribe an old woman and her grandson, a boy about sixteen years old. These people had no relations and were very poor. They were so poor that they were despised by the rest of the tribe. They had nothing of their own, and always, after the village started to move the camp from one place to another, these two would stay behind the rest, to look over the old camp, and pick up anything that the other Indians had thrown away, as worn-out or useless. In this way, they would sometimes get pieces of robes, worn-out moccasins with holes in them, and bits of meat.

Now, it happened one day, after the tribe had moved away from the camp, that this old woman and her boy were following along the trail behind the rest, when they came to a miserable old worn-out dun horse, which they supposed had been abandoned by some Indians. He was thin and exhausted, was blind of one eye, had a sore back, and one of his forelegs was very much swollen. In fact, he was so worthless that none of the Pawnees had been willing to take the trouble to try to drive him along with them. But when the old woman and her boy came along, the boy said, "Come now, we will take this old horse, for we can make him carry our pack." So the old woman put her pack on the horse, and drove him along, but he limped and could only go very slowly.

The tribe moved up on the North Platte, until they came

to Court House Rock. The two poor Indians followed them, and camped with the others. One day while they were here, the young men who had been sent out to look for buffalo, came hurrying into camp and told the chiefs that a large herd of buffalo was near, and that among them was a spotted calf.

The head chief of the Pawnees had a very beautiful daughter, and when he heard about the spotted calf, he ordered his old crier to go about through the village, and call out that the man who killed the spotted calf should have his daughter for his wife. For a spotted robe is *ti-war-uks-ti*—big medicine.

The buffalo were feeding about four miles from the village, and the chiefs decided that the charge should be made from there. In this way, the man who had the fastest horse would be the most likely to kill the calf. Then all the warriors and the young men picked out their best and fastest horses, and made ready to start. Among those who prepared for the charge was the poor boy on the old dun horse. But when they saw him, all the rich young braves on their fast horses pointed at him, and said, "Oh, see! There is the horse that is going to catch the spotted calf." And they laughed at him, so that the poor boy was ashamed, and rode off to one side of the crowd, where he could not hear their jokes and laughter.

When he had ridden off some little way, the horse stopped, and turned his head round, and spoke to the boy. He said, "Take me down to the creek, and plaster me all over with mud. Cover my head and neck and body and legs." When the boy heard the horse speak, he was afraid; but he did as he was told. Then the horse said, "Now mount, but do not ride back to the warriors, who laugh at you because you have such a poor horse. Stay right here, until the word is given to charge." So the boy stayed there.

And presently all the fine horses were drawn up in line, and pranced about, and were so eager to go that their riders could hardly hold them in. At last the old crier gave the word, "*Loo-ah*—Go!" Then the Pawnees all leaned forward on their horses and yelled, and away they went. Suddenly, away off to the right was seen the old dun horse. He did not seem to run. He seemed to sail along like a bird. He passed all the fastest horses, and in a moment he was among the buffalo. First he picked out the spotted calf, and charging up alongside of it, *U-ra-rish!* straight flew the arrow. The calf fell. The boy drew another arrow, and killed a fat cow that was running by. Then he dismounted and began to skin the calf, before any of the other warriors had come up. But when the rider got off the old dun horse, how changed he was! He pranced about and would hardly stand still near the dead buffalo. His back was all right again; his legs were well and fine; and both his eyes were clear and bright.

The boy skinned the calf and the cow that he had killed; then he packed all the meat on the horse, put the spotted robe on top of the load, and started back to the camp on foot, leading the dun horse. But even with this heavy load the horse pranced all the time, and was scared at everything he saw. On the way to camp, one of the rich young chiefs of the tribe rode up to the boy, and offered him twelve good horses for the spotted robe, so that he could marry the head chief's beautiful daughter; but the boy laughed at him and would not sell the robe.

Now, while the boy walked to the camp leading the dun horse, most of the warriors rode back, and one of those that came first to the village went to the old woman and said to her, "Your grandson has killed the spotted calf." The old woman said, "Why do you come to tell me this? You ought to be ashamed to make fun of my boy because he is poor." The warrior said, "What I have told you is true," and then he rode away. After a little while another brave rode up to the old woman and said to her, "Your grandson has killed the spotted calf." Then the old woman began to cry, she felt so badly because everyone made fun of her boy because he was poor.

Pretty soon the boy came along, leading the horse up to

the lodge where he and his grandmother lived. It was a little lodge, just big enough for two, and was made up of old pieces of skin that the old woman had picked up, and was tied together with strings of rawhide and sinew. It was the crudest and worst lodge in the village. When the old woman saw her boy leading the dun horse with the load of meat and the robes on it, she was much surprised. The boy said to her, "Here, I have brought you plenty of meat to eat, and here is a robe that you may have for yourself. Take the meat off the horse." Then the old woman laughed, for her heart was glad. But when she went to take the meat from the horse's back, he snorted and jumped about, and acted like a wild horse. The old woman looked at him in wonder, and could hardly believe that it was the same horse. So the boy had to take off the meat, for the horse would not let the old woman come near him.

That night the horse spoke again to the boy and said, "*Wa-ti-hes Chah-ra-rat wa-ta.* Tomorrow the Sioux are coming—a large war party. They will attack the village, and you will have a great battle. Now, when the Sioux are drawn up in line of battle, and are all ready to fight, you jump on me. Ride as hard as you can right into the middle of the Sioux and up to their head chief, their greatest warrior, and count coup* on him and kill him, and then ride back. Do this four times, and count coup on four of the bravest Sioux and kill them, but don't go again. If you go the fifth time, maybe you will be killed, or else you will lose me. *La-ku-ta-chix*—remember." So the boy promised.

The next day it happened as the horse had said, and the Sioux came down and formed a line of battle. Then the boy took his bow and arrows, and jumped on the dun horse, and charged into the midst of them. When the Sioux saw that he was going to strike their head chief,

---

*Among some Plains tribes of North American Indians, the act of striking or touching an enemy in warfare with the hand or at close quarters, as with a short stick, counts as an act of bravery.

they all shot their arrows at him, and the arrows flew so thickly across each other that he sky became dark, but none of them hit the boy. He counted coup on the chief and killed him, and then rode back. After that he charged again among the Sioux, where they were gathered thickest, and counted coup on their bravest warrior and killed him. Then twice more he charged until he had gone four times, as the horse had told him.

But the Sioux and the Pawnees kept on fighting, and the boy stood around and watched the battle. At last he said to himself, "I have been four times and have killed four Sioux, and I am all right. I am not hurt anywhere. Why may I not go again?" So he jumped on the dun horse and charged again. But when he got among the Sioux, one Sioux warrior drew an arrow and shot. The arrow struck the dun horse behind the forelegs and pierced him through, and the horse fell down dead. But the boy jumped off, and fought his way through the Sioux, and ran away as fast as he could to the Pawnees. Now, as soon as the horse was killed, the Sioux said to each other, "This horse was like a man. He was a brave. He was not like a horse." And they took their knives and hatchets, and hacked the dun horse and gashed his flesh, and cut him into small pieces.

The Pawnees and Sioux fought all day long, but toward night the Sioux broke and fled.

The boy felt very badly that he had lost his horse; and after the fight was over, he went out from the village to where it had taken place, to mourn for his horse. He went to the spot where the horse lay, and gathered up all the pieces of flesh, which the Sioux had cut off, and the legs and the hoofs, and put them all together in a pile. Then he went to the top of a hill near by, and sat down and drew his robe over his head, and began to mourn for his horse.

As he sat there, he heard a great windstorm coming up; it passed over him with a loud rushing sound, and after the wind came rain. The boy looked down, from where he sat, to the pile of flesh and bones, which was all that was left of his horse, and he could just see it through the rain. The rain passed by, but his heart was heavy, and he kept on mourning.

Pretty soon came another rushing wind and, after it, rain. As he looked through the driving rain toward the spot where the pieces lay, he thought that they seemed to come together and take shape, and that the pile looked like a horse lying down, but he could not see well for the thick rain.

After this came a third storm like the others. Now when he looked toward the horse he thought he saw its tail move from side to side two or three times, and that it lifted its head from the ground. The boy was afraid and wanted to run away, but he stayed.

As he waited there came another storm. And through the rain, the boy saw the horse raise himself up on his forelegs and look about. Then the dun horse stood up.

The boy left the hilltop, and went down to the horse. When the boy came near to him, the horse spoke and said, "You have seen how it has been this day, and you may know how it will be after this. But Ti-ra-wa has been good, and has let me come back to you. After this, do what I tell you, not any more, not any less. Now lead me off, far away from the camp, behind that big hill. Leave me there tonight, and in the morning come for me." And the boy did as he was told.

When the boy went for the horse in the morning, he found with him a beautiful white gelding, much more handsome than any horse in the tribe. That night the dun horse told the boy to take him again to the place behind the big hill, and to come for him the next morning. When the boy went again, he found with him a beautiful black gelding. So for ten nights he left the horse among the hills, and each morning he found a different horse—a bay, a roan, a gray, a blue, a spotted horse—all of them finer than any horses that the Pawnees had ever had in their tribe before.

Now the boy was rich, and he married the beautiful

daughter of the head chief, and when he became older, he was made head chief himself. He had many children by his beautiful wife, and one day when his oldest boy died, he wrapped him in the spotted-calf robe and buried him in it. He always took good care of his old grandmother, and kept her in his own lodge until she died. The dun horse was never ridden except at feasts, and when they were going to have a doctors' dance, but he was always led about with the chief, wherever he went. The horse lived in the village for many years, until he became very old. And at last he died.